## WINDWALKER

He wanted to run but his limbs were so heavy he couldn't move. The unrelenting wind peppered his eyes and he had to squeeze them shut. After a moment, he forced himself to look at the demons one more time. The figures were still there, behind them dozens of other figures, their hideous faces gauzed by the flying sand.

He pressed his palms against his eyes to block the nightmare. He couldn't open his mouth because of the whirling dust, but in his mind he was screaming: "Stop. *Stop. Stop!*"

Suddenly it came to an end. The silence was deafening.

Williston pulled his palms from his eyes and looked around the room. The sunlight poured through the kiva's door. The wind was gone. The demons had left.

"The *a'doshle* have looked into your heart, Senator Williston," Windwalker said quietly. "They have seen your virtue. You are welcome here."

# LEGEND OF THE DEAD

A SHERIFF LANSING MYSTERY

MICAH S. HACKLER

A Dell Book

Published by
Dell Publishing
a division of
Bantam Doubleday Dell Publishing Group, Inc.
1540 Broadway
New York, New York 10036



ISBN: 0-440-22093-9

Printed in the United States of America

Published simultaneously in Canada

November 1995

10 9 8 7 6 5 4 3 2 1

RAD

To Suzie, my wife.
To Jack, my dad. And to the memory
of Betty "Bets" Hackler, my mom.

## ACKNOWLEDGMENTS

Thanks to George Sewell and Dan Baldwin, *The Factory,* whose criticism and encouragement over a lot of years got me this far. To Nancy Love, my agent, much appreciation for taking me on. And for my editor, Jacob Hoye, thanks for the guidance and support.

## Legend of the Dead

"And the Lord God said, Behold, the man is become as one of us, to know good and evil. . . . Therefore the Lord God sent him forth from the garden of Eden. . . . So he drove out the man; and he placed at the east of the garden Cherubim, and a flaming sword which turned every way, to keep the way of the tree of life."

—Genesis 3:22–24

"Because the Human Beings had thought they too could be as the gods, the *a'doshle* came in a whirlwind. They dried the crops, drove the men from their sacred kivas and erased from the Human Beings the memory of the *Shipap*."

—Anasazi Legend

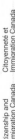

# 1

BEAU FELT A TICKLE IN HIS THROAT. SETTING THE COLEMAN lantern down in the bed of the pickup truck, he reached through the cab window and grabbed the whiskey bottle.

The splash of bourbon burned just right.

"Get your ass out here and help me carry this stuff," Duke barked.

Beau jumped. He was just as grizzled and argumentative as his partner, but not nearly as mean. Beau went out of his way not to cross Duke. He took another quick gulp, screwed the lid back on the bottle, and tossed the whiskey onto the seat.

"I'm coming, dammit," he snorted in feigned bravado.

The New Mexico night was bright with a full moon and countless stars. It was light enough that Beau didn't need to bring the lantern.

Duke had stopped about a hundred yards from the truck. He had set down the four burlap bags he was carrying and tried to catch his breath.

"You're getting to be an old man," Beau joked, picking up two of the bags.

"I can still kick your ass," the older man grunted, picking up the remaining two bags.

Beau knew that was true. He didn't press the issue. "You'll feel better after a shot of whiskey."

"Yeah," Duke wheezed. "You've probably been in the bottle already."

When they reached the truck, Duke set his bags on the tailgate. "Start packing . . . and be careful this time. We lost nearly half the stuff last time."

"Yeah. I know, I know. You told me already. 'Bout a thousand times."

Beau jumped up on the tailgate and lifted the lid on the farthest wooden box. There were six in the truck bed. He lifted out half of the packing paper and set it aside. He then grabbed the nearest burlap bag. Reaching inside, he gingerly pulled out an object wrapped in cloth. Unwrapping the cloth, he extracted a pottery bowl. Holding it close to the lantern, he could see it was still in excellent condition. He started to put it in the bottom of the wooden box.

"Leave those damned things wrapped!" Duke snapped, pulling the whiskey bottle from his lips. "Protects them better."

"We can use this cloth again . . . next time." Beau protested.

"There ain't going to be a next time." Duke took another swig from the bottle. "We've been knocking around out in this desert for twenty years. An odd job here. Mending somebody's fence over there . . . The only time we've ever had any money is when we dig up some dead Indian's pottery. And we ain't gotten much. Well, boy . . . I found out we've been getting paid peanuts for this stuff. . . . That bowl you got in your hand. What do we usually get?"

Beau shrugged. "Ten . . . fifteen bucks."

"We can get a hundred, easy."

Beau was dumbfounded. "Where?"

"Los Angeles, Houston. They got dealers. Art galleries. They'll pay a lot more than some rancher up the road. Hell, that's where they take them. They don't use 'em for nothin'."

"Can't we just take this stuff to Santa Fe? They got art galleries there."

"Santa Fe!" Duke spit. "They'd throw your ass in jail so fast, you'd think you'd raped the governor's wife or somethin'. They'd have a pretty good idea where you got the stuff. Gotta go out of state. Someplace where they won't ask questions."

"Guess it's Los Angeles, then." Beau extended his hand to retrieve the bottle.

Duke took another sip before handing it over. "Why Los Angeles?"

"Remember the trouble we got into in Amarillo last time?" He took a drink and wiped his mouth. "We skipped bail. I'll bet they're just waiting for us to step foot back in Texas."

Duke chuckled. "Yeah, but that was one helluva night, wasn't it?"

Beau started laughing. "Yeah. Remember when you grabbed that barmaid from behind? She must of dropped ten Lone Stars."

Duke grabbed the bottle from his partner. "Just shut up about that. Start packin'."

"Yeah. All right." Beau didn't argue. Duke was mean in general. But he made an even meaner drunk.

Duke walked around the truck, drinking from the bottle and trying to loosen the kinks in his shoulders.

Beau kept busy with his packing. He had packed two boxes and was starting on the third when he got a solid whack along the side of his head.

"You, asshole," Duke growled, half drunk. "Where are the pick and shovel?"

"Hell, Duke," Beau cowered, rubbing his ear. "I thought you had 'em."

"How could I have 'em? I was draggin' four damn sacks full of pots."

"Well, I had three bags and the lantern. . . ."

"Aw, shut up. . . ."

"They must be back at the—"

"Said 'shut up'! I know where they are. Gimme the damn lantern."

Beau obediently handed over the lantern. "You want me to go?"

"No, dammit. I want you to pack the goddamn pots so we can get outta here." Snarling under his breath, Duke stumbled into the night, whiskey bottle in one hand, the lantern in the other.

"Son of a bitch!" Beau growled, still rubbing his ear. "I oughtta kick his ass!" He knew he never would. Somehow, though, just saying it made him feel better.

The range hand climbed out of the truck bed and opened the passenger door to the cab. Under the seat he found another pint of whiskey. He clicked on the radio, already tuned to a country-and-western station.

Sitting on the tailgate, he watched the lantern disappear behind a hill a quarter of a mile away. The whiskey was going down easily. "Yeah, that's just what I'll do," Beau insisted to himself with increasing confidence. "I'm gonna kick his ass."

He tried to calculate how much money they were going to make hauling their booty to Los Angeles, but couldn't. He comforted himself with the thought that math was never his strong suit.

Polishing off the pint, it took him three tries to climb into the truck bed to finish packing the pottery. The moon gave him just enough light.

The quiet night was interrupted by the not too distant howl of a coyote. Beau hated coyotes.

"Get outta here!" he yelled.

The coyote howled again, as if in response.

A little breeze kicked up, rustling the sagebrush around the truck.

"I said, get the hell outta here!" Without thinking,

he threw the pot he was holding at a nearby bush. The pot shattered on the ground. In response, the breeze increased.

Beau jumped from the back of the truck, tripping over the side. He quickly scrambled to his feet and threw the cab door open. Grabbing the carbine from the rifle rack along the back window, he pointed it over the side of the truck, in the direction of the howling coyote.

The breeze had increased to a wind, and sand started pelting him in the face. At the same time clouds obscured the moon and most of the sky.

Suddenly it was very dark.

Beau had to shield his eyes from the stinging sand. The only sound coming to him was the whipping wind. He tried peering in the direction his partner had taken to catch a glimpse of a returning lantern. . . . There was nothing.

In the distance came a muffled scream.

It was an awful sound, a sound that didn't quite seem human. Beau felt a shudder race through his body.

"Duke," Beau bellowed. "Duke. Is that you?"

The wind answered with a howl of its own.

Beau reached behind the truck seat and pulled out a flashlight. When he turned it on, the bulb glowed brightly for a moment, then flickered out. He banged the flashlight against the side of the truck to get it to work. This time the light was dim.

He took a few halting steps into the darkness. He didn't want to lose the truck in the sandstorm.

"Duke! Duke! You damned old bastard, answer me!"

He stopped to listen. The response he got was the snap of a twig only yards from where he stood. He turned his dim beam in that direction, only to have the light flicker out.

In the blowing wind and darkness he sensed movement. He dropped the useless flashlight and raised his rifle. "Who's there?" he demanded. There was no response. But there was movement again, a few feet to the right. Beau shifted his aim, squinting his eyes against the wind, trying to get a better look.

Through the darkness, a tall figure suddenly appeared.

"Stop right there, mister!" Beau ordered.

The shape continued its approach. Behind it and at its sides, two more figures appeared. Beau fired a single shot at the first silhouette. All three shapes continued their march.

Beau kept firing until the magazine was empty. Whimpering with fear, he threw the rifle to the ground and ran for the truck, guided by the sound of the radio. He could feel them close behind him.

The cab door was still open when he reached the truck.

He slammed the door behind him, stomping on the accelerator and turning the key at the same time. The truck lurched and the radio went dead.

"Not now, dammit," he screamed. "Not now!"

He turned the key again but the truck refused to respond. At that moment Beau imagined unseen hands were grabbing for him through the window.

Beau screamed, pulling free of the grasping hands. He slid across the seat, kicking the passenger door open. Jumping into the darkness he waved his hands frantically, beating away the shadows and running for his life.

# 2

SHERIFF CLIFF LANSING TURNED HIS JEEP OFF THE MAIN highway onto the dirt road leading into the hills. The morning air was still clean and crisp and he drove with his window down. In a couple of hours the arid landscape would be baking.

The road was rock strewn and dusty. It was a typical two-rut road common in the back hills, usually used by ranchers looking for stray cattle. Occasionally weekend riders would make the two-hour drive up from Santa Fe, park their horse trailers, and explore the back country for a day. More and more, though, horses were being replaced by four-by-fours. Lansing hated to see that. Motor vehicles tore up the high desert.

He slowed his Jeep to avoid a large rock jutting up in the middle of the road. He still got a pretty good bump. The microphone to his radio bounced out of its cradle. Lansing caught it before it hit the floor.

"Slow down, Roscoe," he said out loud. "Wherever you're going will still be there even if you're late."

Lansing downshifted to climb a small hill. At the top he stopped to survey the land. The highway sat below and behind him about five miles away. The road in front of him disappeared into the hills to the east.

He pulled out his binoculars to scan the landscape. Searching left to right, he slowly panned the hills. It took a moment before he found his quarry. A couple of miles away the cab of a red pickup truck poked up above a hill.

Engaging gears, Lansing continued, carefully avoiding the more dangerous rocks. The red truck had taken an even smaller trail than the dirt road Lansing had been following.

The sheriff parked several yards from the truck. He didn't want to disturb the area around the scene. As he approached the truck, he could hear country music coming from the radio. The driver's door was closed. The passenger door was wide open. Inside the cab, the keys were still in the ignition.

Lansing opened the door and slipped into the seat. He tried the engine. It started on the first try. He shut it down, then turned off the radio.

Outside the truck, he checked the back. There were six wooden crates in the bed. He lifted the lid on one. It was full of shredded newspapers, obviously being used for packing material. He dug through the papers. There was nothing else in the crate.

He checked the next one. Still nothing.

It was the same in each box.

On the tailgate he found an empty whiskey pint.

Puzzled, Lansing scratched the back of his head. This wasn't what he expected to find.

Lansing pushed his Stetson a little farther back on his head and began looking around on the ground. *For what?* he thought. *What should I be looking for?*

He began a semicircular search pattern starting at the back of the truck. A few yards away he found the shattered remains of what had been Indian pottery. To Lansing it looked as though it had been very old. He left the pot shards where he found them and continued his search.

Twenty yards from the truck he found a rifle. Next to the rifle were a flashlight and several spent cartridges. He left the items on the ground, untouched, and continued his pattern.

The desert had its own distinct sounds. The night desert had its coyotes, owls, and crickets. The day desert had the clackity-clack of roadrunners and buzzing of insects. To Lansing, the buzz of insects seemed more pronounced than normal. Instinctively, he followed the sound.

Thirty feet from the rifle, hidden by a low tuft of sage, was the body of a man lying faceup. Flies were swarming around the body, crawling in and out of the nose and the gaping mouth, feeding on the blotches of dried blood on the man's chest. He had been shot a half dozen times. Next to the body was an empty whiskey bottle.

Lansing shook his head, turned and headed back to his Jeep.

"Marilyn, this is Cliff Lansing," the sheriff said into the microphone. "Can you hear me okay?"

"Sure can, Sheriff," came the response over the radio a moment later. "You find that truck you were looking for?"

"Yeah, sure did. . . ."

"How 'bout those bogeymen Beau Watson was jabbering about?" Marilyn interrupted.

"No. No bogeymen out here. Is Beau still back in the interrogation room?"

"Yes, sir."

"Have Joe put him back in the drunk tank. I don't want him wandering off. I also need you to dispatch Stu with the forensic kit and an ambulance."

"Somebody hurt?"

"No. Somebody's dead. Duke Semple. Have the ambulance follow Stu. Tell him I'll meet them on Highway Twelve, ten miles south of the crossroads. . . . And tell them to step on it. It's getting hot out here."

Lansing rummaged around the back of his Jeep. Under his toolbox he found an army blanket. After covering Duke's body, the sheriff carefully backed his Jeep around and headed for the highway to meet his deputy.

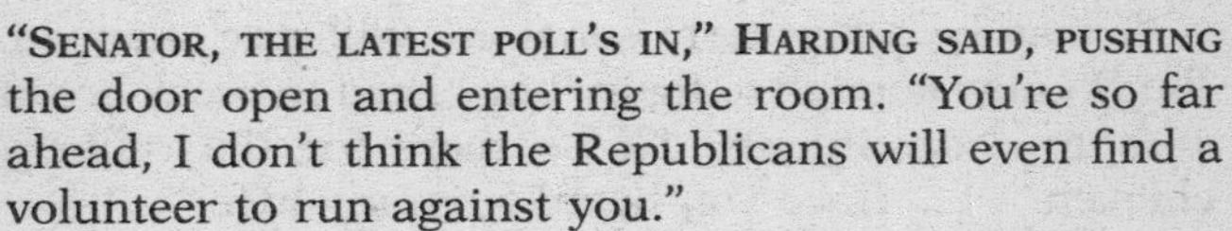

# 3

"SENATOR, THE LATEST POLL'S IN," HARDING SAID, PUSHING the door open and entering the room. "You're so far ahead, I don't think the Republicans will even find a volunteer to run against you."

He plopped the folders he was carrying on the conference table behind the senator. "And here are the summaries of the impact study you asked for."

Carter Williston sat gazing out the window, his back to the door. He didn't bother to turn around. "Why are you so wrapped up in polls, Harding? The primaries are a year away."

"It's my job, Carter," the aide responded, sounding a little miffed. "I'm your chief of staff. I'm supposed to worry about things like that."

"You're also supposed to worry about my schedule," Carter snapped, finally swiveling his seat around. "This attorney I had to meet was supposed to be here fifteen minutes ago."

"His office called. He was held up in court. He should be here any minute now."

Williston stood and started pacing. He looked the part of a distinguished senator: striking silver hair, a slim build, immaculately dressed in a custom-made suit.

"I don't like waiting, Harding. It's already ten o'clock. I have a luncheon with the Santa Fe Rotary, golf with the governor this afternoon, a dedication banquet tonight. I wanted at least an hour of peace and quiet this morning. I haven't had a moment to myself since we hit Albuquerque three days ago."

"Senator, please," Harding pleaded, "this meeting with Longtree shouldn't take more than ten minutes. Your limo is waiting behind the Federal Building. We can have you back in your hotel by ten-thirty.

"I've already talked to the Rotary Club. If you want to skip the rubbery chicken and just show up for your speech, it's all right with them."

"I may be a first-term senator," Williston snapped, "but I know enough to figure out I need to break bread with my constituents. I'll be there for the rubbery chicken. . . . Have you heard from my wife?"

"No, sir. Should I have Judy try to reach her?"

"What do you think?"

"Yes, sir." Harding started backing out of the room. "Is there anything else?"

"Yes," Williston grumbled. "Knock before you walk in on me next time."

"Yes, Senator." Harding hurried up and left.

With no great degree of conviction, Williston opened the top folder in front of him. The title of the report read: SUMMARY, ENVIRONMENTAL IMPACT STUDY, LAND TRANSFER TO ZUNI NATION. The report had been prepared by the Bureau of Land Management. Williston was very familiar with the findings. The Bureau of Land Management was going to give 150,000 acres of property to the Zuni reservation in Arizona and New Mexico. In exchange, the Zunis had to relinquish all claims to 150,000 acres of disputed territory in northern New Mexico. The new property was fallow grazing land and desert. The disputed property was fallow grazing land and hill country.

After three hundred pages of describing the land in question, what it looked like, how it was used, how it would be used in the future, the report finally made its conclusion: there would be no significant impact to the physical environment in either state, but there would be significant benefits to the Zuni nation if the land transfer took place.

That made sense to Williston. It had taken a lot of legislative finesse to pull it off. The Arizona delegation wasn't thrilled at giving up any land. It helped that no one lived on the territory they would surrender. No constituents to upset. Of course, Williston and his delegation had to promise to support some unnamed proposal that would come to a vote in the future. But that was easy. That was politics.

Even the secretary of the interior rolled over on the issue.

Everyone was for the proposal—except the Zuni nation.

There was a knock at the door.

"Come in," Williston ordered.

The door opened. Harding ushered in a man in his early thirties carrying a briefcase. Williston stood.

"Senator Williston," Harding said by way of introduction. "Francis Longtree."

Longtree extended his hand. "It's good to meet you, Senator. But if you don't mind, I'd rather go by Frank."

Williston shook the proffered hand and sized up his visitor. Longtree was definitely of Native American extract. He had strong, handsome racial features: high cheekbones, a red-earth complexion, black hair. He also had a firm handshake.

"I'm sorry I'm late," Longtree continued. "The court proceedings ran a little long."

"Sounds like a Senate hearing," Williston joked, trying to put his visitor at ease. "Please sit down." He indicated a chair close to his own.

Longtree sat, as did Williston. Harding closed the door and took his position standing next to it.

"I'm going to get right to the point, Frank," Williston began, avoiding the usual niceties he exercised during a first meeting. "Before the federal government started acting on the land-swap proposal with the Zuni nation, we went to your tribal council and asked if they were interested. A year ago everyone was for it. Your folks said they could use the extra land for a hundred different projects. Half the council didn't even know they had claims on land in northern New Mexico.

"*Now,* all of a sudden, after Congress has spent nearly a half million dollars on an environmental impact study, the Zuni Tribal Council wants to renege on the transfer. Don't you people realize you're going to gain land worth millions of dollars?"

"For starters, Senator, I would prefer that you didn't refer to the Zuni nation as 'you people.'" The attorney sounded ruffled. "Second, no one has reneged on any deal.

"Senator, you have to understand, the Zunis are not a rich people. The influenza epidemic this past winter took a terrible toll, both physically and spiritually. There are some in the tribe who believe we are a dying people. That the illness that visited us is just the beginning.

"Although I am not a member of the tribal council, I am their legal representative. As their representative, I have recommended that they accept the offer. I personally believe it will restore hope to people who have lost hope. However, despite my recommendations and in spite of their own inclinations, the council members are deferring their decision until the Watcher has made his decision."

Williston looked to Harding, who shrugged. "Who is

this 'Watcher' individual?" Williston asked, opening his hands, palms up, in perplexed dismay.

"He is the caretaker, so to speak, of the Anasazi Strip. He lives in the hills around there. Kind of keeps an eye on it. Protects it."

"What? Like a forest ranger?" Harding asked.

"In some respects, I suppose." Longtree nodded. "But his main concerns tend toward the spiritual."

"So he's a medicine man?" the senator queried.

"He is not a medicine man. In our tongue he is called *Kiaklo,*" the attorney corrected. "He is the keeper of our history. He remembers the ancient ways and passes them on to younger generations."

"Okay, now that we're finished with the semantics lesson," Williston quipped, "what does this *Kiaklo* have to do with the decision of the council?"

"What is called the Anasazi Strip has been a part of the Zuni heritage since before time can be remembered. Before the time of the white man the ancestors of the Zuni fought great battles with the Navajo, the Pueblo, even the Aztecs to protect that sacred ground."

"We appreciate your people's ties to the land," Harding interrupted. "But the argument that some piece of land is sacred has been put forth by every Indian tribe on this continent. If the Indian nations had their way, this entire country would be declared sacred and handed back to them."

Longtree glared at the senatorial aide.

Williston intervened, giving his assistant a warning scowl. "That's a philosophical question we don't need to deal with right now, Harding." The response on Harding's face told the senator there would be no more interruptions. Williston turned his attention back to the attorney. "You were saying about the sacred ground . . ."

"Many people in the Zuni tribe have forgotten that they have descended from the Anasazi or that the

Anasazi Strip is an important part of their heritage. Even the elders forget. But the Watcher is there and he reminds them."

"You're evading the issue, counselor," Williston pressed. "Is the Watcher going to go along with the proposal?"

Longtree shook his head. "I don't know. He won't tell me. He wants to talk to you."

"Fine," Williston stood. "Bring him in."

"He's not here. He's at home. He wants you to come see him."

"I'm afraid that's out of the question," Williston responded. "I'm a very busy man. I don't have time to drop everything so I can run around the hills and talk to some malcontent."

"*Kiaklo* is not a malcontent. He is a very wise man. He knows your office first introduced this proposal of a land swap. He knows you pushed through the legislation. He knows, whatever your reasons are, you want this thing to happen very much. That is why he knows you will come visit him."

Williston looked at his watch. He was impatient and very annoyed. "I'll have to let you know, Mr. Longtree. Right now I have to get ready for a luncheon."

Abruptly Williston started for the door. "Harding, you have his number. . . ." Williston stopped briefly at the door the aide was now holding open. "My office will be in touch."

Williston left the room followed by his aide, leaving Longtree alone.

# 4

LANSING SLOWED HIS JEEP WHEN HE REACHED THE CORPORAtion limits of Las Palmas. Two blocks into town he turned in to the Phillips 66 station. The owner, Ed Rodriguez, came running out. Ed had been operating the station since Lansing was a kid. He was as much a fixture of the community as the courthouse.

"What's the problem, Mr. Rodriguez?" Lansing asked, rolling down the window, the engine still running. "Marilyn told me you had some trouble."

"Those two Indians . . . the ones that always come into town and get drunk . . . They're in the alley behind my station." The old man gestured with his thumb. "I told them to leave. The man, he pulls a knife. He tells me go away or he'll cut me."

"Did he try to cut you?"

"No, but he said he would."

"Do you want to press charges?"

"No. I don't want no trouble. I just want them to go."

"Okay, Mr. Rodriguez. I'll take care of it." The sheriff shifted into first gear and edged his Jeep around the corner of the station.

Lying on the ground, leaning against the trash Dumpster and each other, were a man and a woman:

Jonathan Akee and his common-law wife, Susan. They were common fixtures in Las Palmas, too, Lansing thought. Once a month, when Jonathan's VA check came in, they would hitch a ride into town from the reservation and drink themselves silly.

Lansing had warned them in the past about not becoming public nuisances. Previously, Jonathan and Susan would pass out on the main street or in the doorway of some business. In the past year or so they had been pretty good about restricting their activities to the back alleys.

Lansing knelt near Akee, but out of arms' reach, just in case he did have a knife.

"Jonathan." Lansing spoke in a loud voice. "You awake?"

The Indian mumbled something, brushing away the sound of Lansing's voice as if it had been a fly.

"Jonathan!" Lansing yelled.

Akee jerked awake. "What . . . what? What do you want?"

"It's Sheriff Lansing, Jonathan. I stopped off to see if you and Susan are all right."

Akee rubbed his eyes, then turned to the sheriff. "All right?" he asked.

Jonathan's speech was slurred. Lansing suspected Akee wasn't sure where he was. "You got a knife on you, Jonathan?"

"Who? Me?" Akee tried to focus on the question. "I think I got a knife." He felt around his chest and waist, then on the ground around him. He found the knife between himself and his wife. He picked it up. "Yeah, see? I got a knife."

"Can I see it?" Lansing held out his hand.

"Sure, Sheriff"—Jonathan handed over the knife—"but you gotta give it back."

"Don't worry, Jonathan. I will." Lansing tossed the knife into the front seat of his Jeep.

"You two feel like taking a ride?" Lansing knelt next to Susan. She smelled like very cheap wine. Thunderbird, Lansing suspected. She was still out cold.

"I don't know." Jonathan shook his head slowly. "She got sick last night." He pointed to the Dumpster they were leaning against.

"Tell you what. We'll ride with the windows down, just in case she gets sick again." Lansing took one of Susan's arms. "Can you help me get her into my Jeep?"

Jonathan grunted, indicating he could. The two men half dragged, half carried the unconscious Indian woman to the backseat of the sheriff's Jeep. "Why don't you ride back there with her, Jonathan, just in case she needs some help?"

Jonathan nodded compliantly, in no condition to argue.

It was already late morning when Lansing parked his patrol Jeep next to the courthouse. There was no shade anywhere to give his two charges in the backseat any relief. They wouldn't have to sit out there long. The sheriff entered the wing of the courthouse housing his office.

The San Phillipe County Courthouse was a multifunctional complex. Built in 1908, it housed the sheriff's department, all court facilities, the assessor's office, the offices for the board of education and the county library. The only other county building in town was for the department of roads. That was a combination office building and garage on the outskirts of town.

The municipal building for the city of Las Palmas was a single-story building sitting across the town square from the courthouse. Las Palmas was too small to have its own police department, so Lansing's office was the single source of law and order for the entire county.

Lansing entered his department. Along the outside wall of the reception area were a couple of wooden chairs and an old wooden table strewn with brochures and magazines. On the opposite wall was the counter. That was Marilyn's station. It served as the communication center, secretarial desk, and reception center.

Marilyn was a plump, jolly woman of an age vaguely between fifty-five and sixty-five. Her hair was white. Her skin was a glowing, healthy pink. She was energetic and helpful. She was the earth-mother of the sheriff's department and the heart of the operations. Back when her husband was still alive she always brought in grocery bags full of vegetables they had grown in their garden. The vegetables were handed out to anyone happening into the sheriff's office, sometimes even to prisoners. Since Toby had passed away, though, Marilyn limited herself to growing flowers. When they were in season, she always kept a vase of fresh blooms on her counter. That day's bouquet was yellow roses.

"Did you stop at the Phillips Sixty-six station?" Marilyn asked, looking up from her typewriter as Lansing entered.

"Sure did." Lansing smiled, removing his Stetson. "He was having a little trouble with Jonathan Akee and his wife."

"Drunk again." Marilyn nodded knowingly. "I suppose it is that time of month.

"Joe Cortez is back in the day room. Beau is still sleeping it off in his cell. Everything else is quiet."

"You don't need me around here," Lansing kidded. "I may as well go fishing. You can call me if you need anything."

"That won't work," Marilyn said with a laugh. "You don't like fishing."

"I could learn to like it." Lansing continued past the reception counter to the door leading to the back offices. Before going through the door he turned back to Marilyn. "Give Santa Fe a call and see how long it would take to get a coroner up here."

Deputy Joe Cortez sat in the day room sipping a cup of coffee and reading a stack of reports.

"What've you got there?" Lansing asked, walking over to the coffeepot to check if it was still hot.

"Monthly crime stats from Santa Fe. Came in this morning's mail." He noticed the sheriff checking the pot. "Should still be hot. I just unplugged it."

Lansing nodded, pouring himself a cup.

"What's this I heard about Duke Semple?"

"Dead. Shot up pretty good too." Lansing took a sip of coffee. The coffee was old and tasted bad. He poured the coffee back into the pot. "You made this coffee, didn't you, Joe?"

"The pot was empty. I had to make some."

"I told you"—Lansing pointed a threatening finger —"you don't make the coffee around here. If we run out, let Marilyn make it. You're a damned good deputy, Joe, but you don't know the first thing about making coffee."

"Yes, sir," Cortez said sheepishly. "What happened out there with Duke and Beau?"

"You heard Beau's story this morning. I think it hovers around the truth. Two old ranch hands got drunk, one of them shot the other. Pretty cut and dried. Stu's out there gathering up the evidence.

"Listen, I have Jonathan and Susan Akee out in the back of my patrol car. They're both drunk, but she's in pretty bad shape. How 'bout driving them out to the reservation for me? Take them straight to the clinic. Marilyn will let them know you're on your way."

"Sure thing," Cortez said, standing.

"Go ahead and use my car." He tossed the deputy his keys. "I need to talk to our guest."

"Okay," Joe responded, grabbing his hat from a wall peg. "Check in with you later."

"Joe," the sheriff called after him. "Be sure Jonathan gets his knife back. It's on my front seat."

Lansing walked to the back of the offices, where the jail was located. There were only three cells, usually reserved for drunks. Beau Watson was the only occupant. He lay on his back on one of the beds with his arm across his face.

"Beau!" Lansing called out. "You awake yet?"

"Yeah," the ranch hand responded, not moving his arm. "What do you want?"

"I want to ask you some questions about last night."

Watson refused to move. "I'm hungry."

"I'll get you something to eat in a minute. I want you to tell me about last night first."

"I already told you and your deputy what happened, Sheriff. Right now I want something to eat."

"You got any money on you, Beau?"

"No."

"I'll make you a deal. You tell me again about what happened last night, and I'll get you something to eat. Otherwise, I'm going to kick you out of my jail right now and you can go hungry."

"Son of a bitch," Beau growled, sitting up in the bunk. "All right. I'll tell you just like it happened. . . ."

# 5

"SENATOR WILLISTON." THE ELEGANTLY DRESSED MATRON extended her hand. "I've been looking all over, but I haven't seen your lovely wife anywhere."

Williston smiled pleasantly. "You know how involved she is with her volunteer work. She had to cut short her visit to New Mexico to handle an emergency in Washington."

Williston knew that was a lie. Karen hated New Mexico. She was an Easterner, much more at home with the cramped sophistication of Washington, D.C., or New York than with the wide-open casualness of the West.

They had met when he was a midshipman at Annapolis. She was a debutante from a long line of Baltimore aristocrats. He was her escort at her debut. It was love at first sight. They were married the June he graduated from the academy. He was the ideal officer. She was the ideal officer's wife. She had been bred for the role.

But the years had taken a heavy toll. The marriage was childless and their personal relationship had been placed on the back burner for the sake of his career. But after thirty years of faithful service he never made it beyond the rank of captain. In a way, he blamed

Karen for that. He wanted a shipboard command. She insisted he take Pentagon assignments. Fifteen of his thirty years had been spent in Washington.

"I do understand how that is." The woman smiled. "You know, I tell all my friends how fortunate it is you decided to return to New Mexico after your naval career. . . ."

That was a fluke, Williston thought. He had kept up ties with his native state, but he had never planned on returning. Captain Carter Williston, U.S.N., had every intention of remaining in Washington, D.C. It's what his wife wanted.

It was Merrill McGaffrey who suggested the soon to be retired naval officer could have his cake and eat it too. The senior senator from New Mexico, Roger Burns, would not be running for reelection. If Williston was interested, the door was open . . . and McGaffrey was holding it for him.

It took a lot of talking, but Carter eventually persuaded his wife to move to Albuquerque to establish their residency. Williston assumed a position as senior consultant in one of McGaffrey's companies. He and his wife attended all the right functions, cultivated all the right friendships. When Burns announced he would not seek reelection, Williston was in place. He had no skeletons in his closet, but he was a Washington insider. He had not been tainted by politics, but he had thirty years' proven service to his country. He was the ideal candidate.

Within a year of moving to New Mexico, Carter and Karen Williston were back in Washington, this time as Senator and Mrs. Williston.

"I consider myself the fortunate one." Williston smiled. "If you would excuse me, I need to speak to Merrill McGaffrey."

"Certainly, Senator," the matron said graciously.

Williston weaved his way through the crowd.

The opening of the new Museum of the Americas was a formal, black-tie affair. The museum was going to be the largest repository of Native American artifacts and artwork in the world. It would eventually rival the collections in the Smithsonian and the National Galleria in Mexico City. The senator had been told it would be a monument to his vision and foresight. Williston saw it as a tax write-off for his benefactor, Merrill McGaffrey.

McGaffrey had donated the land, the building materials, and over one hundred pieces of artwork from his personal collection. Amortized over ten years, McGaffrey and the IRS had settled on a total donation estimated at eleven million dollars. Williston guessed the actual value at one million, one point five million—maybe. But not eleven million.

Merrill McGaffrey stood in front of one of the many Aztec displays. This particular display was a scale-model representation of pre-Columbian Tenochtitlán, the Aztec capital of Montezuma. At the center of the city was a double pyramid, complete with supplicants worshipping the human sacrifices taking place. A large group of men and women listened intently to McGaffrey's lecture.

"The Aztecs were the North American equivalent of the Mongol hordes of Asia. They wandered the American Southwest for nearly three hundred years before settling in Central Mexico. They mingled with the desert tribes of New Mexico, Arizona, Nevada; borrowed from them, conquered them, corrupted their religions, and moved on.

"As magnificent as their culture was, the centerpiece of their religion and the one thing that tainted European attitudes toward Native Americans for two hundred years was human sacrifice. On the left there" —he pointed to one of the pyramids—"is the temple to their god of the sun and war, Huitzilopochtli. He had a voracious appetite and thousands were sacrificed every year. The bodies of the sacrificial victims were simply tossed down the stone steps. The still-beating hearts were placed on stone altars like this one." A few of the elegantly dressed women gasped. McGaffrey placed his hand on a crouching, stone-carved jaguar next to the display. An ornate bowl was cut into the back of the figure to receive the hearts. "This is a duplicate of the stone altar found in Mexico City. It's seven feet long and weighs six tons."

"You mean with your money you couldn't get the original, Mack?" one of the men in the crowd asked, laughing.

"I have the original, Fred, but it was too heavy to move. It's at home. . . . I use it for a birdbath!"

Williston didn't hear the exchange between McGaffrey and the man. All he caught was the burst of laughter from the crowd.

Individuals on the outskirts of the group noticed the senator approaching. They parted to let the politician pass. It was as though Moses had orchestrated the gathering. Within a few seconds a path had been cleared between Williston and McGaffrey.

"And here's the man of the hour," McGaffrey announced, gesturing with an empty cocktail glass. "A good friend to Santa Fe and true son of New Mexico, Senator Carter Williston."

The crowd around Williston burst into applause. Several people near the senator shook his hand or slapped him on the back with congratulations.

"No, no," the senator protested. "Really. I only did what any one of you would have done for this great state. You all should know who is really responsible for this evening: William Jefferson!"

The people surrounding Williston looked at each other in bewilderment. The senator could tell the big question was, "Who the hell is William Jefferson?"

"Yes," Williston continued, "William Jefferson. The director of the Internal Revenue Service. If he hadn't approved all those donations for tax exemption, we might still be waiting on Mack McGaffrey to write that first check."

The crowd burst into laughter, as if on cue. Williston looked at McGaffrey. The millionaire was laughing too. McGaffrey had a tough facade though. The senator couldn't tell if he was amused.

"Come on, Senator," McGaffrey said jovially, taking him by the arm. "Let me buy you a drink. You can tell me about your golf game with the governor."

Williston allowed himself to be led away.

Even though they were the same age, McGaffrey looked to be older. He was an inch or two taller than Williston and outweighed him by forty pounds.

"That was real funny about the IRS, Carter." McGaffrey didn't sound amused. "You should have saved that one for the banquet later. That way everybody could have enjoyed it."

"Mack, it was just a joke. Lighten up. Everyone here knows this whole affair is because of what you put into it."

"Yeah, and I don't want them to forget it either." McGaffrey grabbed two champagne cocktails from a passing waitress. He handed one to the senator. "Have the police broken up those protesters outside?"

"I don't know. The governor said he was going to talk to them. This is a free country and they are entitled to their point of view."

"If those Indians out there had their way, they'd take every item out of this museum and stick it back in the ground."

"It's their heritage, Mack. We've taken everything else from them. They feel as though they have a right to preserve their past in their own way. It's part of their religion."

McGaffrey squeezed his finger and thumb together. "I care about that much for their religion."

"A lot of people have made a lot of money dealing in Indian artifacts. Illegally. I think those protesters want that kind of desecration stopped."

"What's that supposed to mean?"

"Nothing, Mack. Nothing at all."

McGaffrey took the offensive in the conversation. "I talked with your man, Harding, this afternoon. It sounds like things didn't go well with that Indian attorney this morning."

"He wants me to talk to some old medicine man up in the hills."

"Talk about what?"

"I guess I'm supposed to convince him that this land swap is a good deal for the Zuni nation. This guy evidently doesn't buy it, but without his approval the tribal council won't go along."

"What's the hang-up?"

"He won't come down from his perch. He wants me to come to him."

"Then it sounds to me like it's time for you to visit the mountain, Muhammad." McGaffrey downed his drink in a single gulp. "Do you see a problem with that?"

"I have a schedule, Mack. I've got meetings back in Washington."

"Cancel them," McGaffrey ordered. "Those meetings won't mean a damned thing to you if this land swap doesn't go through."

"Is that a threat, Mack?"

"I don't make threats, Carter. I put you in office. I'll yank you out. Go ask Roger Burns, if you don't think I can't."

Williston sized up his adversary. The old adage "If it sounds too good to be true, it probably is" came to mind. Carter knew when he ran for office that there would have to be paybacks. The navy had its own brand of politics. He played that game for thirty years. But the navy couldn't touch the professionals. Yes, Carter knew there would be paybacks. He just didn't think he'd end up being somebody's lapdog.

"Okay, Mack. I'll arrange things with my staff in the morning."

"That's my boy." McGaffrey slapped him on the back. "I knew we wouldn't have any problems." He started to walk away, then stopped. "And Carter. It really is bad form not having your wife here. I wouldn't let that happen again."

Yes, Karen hated New Mexico. She hated McGaffrey even more. At least Williston understood that one.

# 6

LANSING WALKED ACROSS THE TOWN SQUARE TO THE LAS PALmas Diner. There were three places to eat in town: the diner, the Dixie Queen and Paco's Canteen. The canteen had good Mexican food, but it was at the north end of town. The Dixie Queen was all right for burgers, but the diner had a real menu to order from and served three meals a day. It was also the most popular place to eat, mostly because the location was ideal: next door to the town's municipal building and across the square from the courthouse.

"Hello, Sheriff," Velma said in as coy a voice as she could muster. "It's not lunchtime. You come over to see me?"

"No." The sheriff smiled, taking a seat at the counter. "Not this time. Just came over for some coffee."

"Joe over there making coffee again?" Kelly asked. Kelly was Velma's partner behind the counter.

"No. I told him yesterday I'd fire him if he made another pot. I just needed a break from the office."

Velma turned the cup in front of Lansing right side up and filled it with coffee. "You know, Cliff, if you really need a break, I know just what to do."

"Oh, I know, Velma. You've told me that before."

"You haven't done anything about it."

"Leave him alone, Velma," Kelly ordered, coming to the sheriff's rescue. "Let him enjoy his coffee in peace."

Velma turned away in a huff.

"What're you going to do with Beau Watson, Cliff?" Kelly asked.

"I have to hold him till the county attorney decides what he wants to do."

"You found the body. It was murder, wasn't it?"

"I don't know about that." Cliff took a sip of his coffee. "If it was premeditated, it could be murder. But I don't think it was. I think those two went out, got drunk, and got into a fight."

"I heard Beau said they were attacked by monsters."

"Who told you that?"

"Just about everybody in town."

"Hard to keep a secret in Las Palmas, isn't it? Stu and I both looked around the area up there in the hills. I didn't find anything that looked like monsters. Just a couple of empty whiskey bottles and a bunch of spent rifle shells."

"I'll bet you those monsters came from one of those bottles," Velma commented from the table she was cleaning.

"I think you're probably right, Velma."

A pickup truck sped past the diner from the north of town. It was going nearly fifty miles an hour and almost didn't make the corner past the town square. The truck fishtailed after making the turn with its tires squealing. The turn only slowed it down slightly. A moment later the truck was speeding toward the parking lot at the courthouse. The screeching brakes could be heard for blocks as it slammed to a halt. The driver jumped from the truck and ran into the courthouse.

Velma, Kelly, and the few patrons in the diner were pressed against the window to see what was going on.

Kelly turned to Lansing, who was sitting with his back to the window sipping his coffee. "Cliff, did you see that?"

"Sure did."

"Aren't you going to do anything?"

"My car's at the courthouse. So's my ticket book."

"Well, that's where the truck stopped," Velma complained. "You can catch 'em over there."

"It was a light green Ford pickup with government plates. Right?"

"I didn't see the plates," Velma confessed.

"Trust me. They were government plates. That was Dr. Carerra. I heard she was looking for me and that she's pissed. I don't have to go after her. She'll be here in a minute."

From the other side of the square came the sound of the truck engine starting up. Less than a minute later the truck skidded to a stop in front of the diner. A short, slim, dark-haired woman in her mid-thirties stepped out of the truck. She slammed the door shut and stomped toward the diner.

Kelly, Velma, and the patrons at the window quickly assumed their previous positions, acting as though nothing out of the ordinary was happening. Dr. Carerra stormed into the diner.

"Sheriff Lansing!"

Cliff looked up from his coffee. "Oh, hi, Dr. Carerra."

"Don't play innocent with me, Sheriff." The doctor stuck her finger in Lansing's face. "You knew I was coming into town to talk to you, and I find you over here hiding."

Lansing looked at Kelly. "We're going to take a booth in the back. Bring us some coffee."

Lansing grabbed the doctor's finger and dragged her to the back part of the diner.

"Let go of me, Lansing," Carerra yelled, hitting his arm and trying to pull away.

The sheriff ignored her until they reached the booth farthest from the door. He sat her down on the bench, let go of her finger, then took a position across the table from her.

"All right, Doctor. What's the problem?"

"Susan Akee. Because of you, she almost died."

"Me! What did I do?"

"You're the one who picked her up off the street yesterday, aren't you?"

"Yes . . . and I had Joe Cortez drive her and Jonathan straight to the reservation. Susan didn't look too well. That's why I had him go to the clinic."

"If she didn't look too well, why didn't you have him take her to the county clinic? She was in a coma, Lansing. I had to have her medevacked to the regional hospital in Farmington."

Sheriff Lansing was on the defensive. "How was I supposed to know? I'm not a doctor."

Kelly arrived with the coffee.

The doctor and sheriff sat in silence as Kelly poured. Lansing told the waitress thanks as she left.

"Lansing, I'm frustrated. I could have run my clinic for three months on what that one evacuation flight will cost. . . ." She sat in silence for a moment, then took a sip of coffee.

"I'm sorry, Doc," the sheriff apologized. "I thought I was doing the right thing. How is Susan?"

"She's resting comfortably now. The doctors in Farmington are checking her for epilepsy. I think it was a syncopal episode brought on by dehydration and too much alcohol. I suppose it could have been worse."

"How so?" Lansing asked, relaxing a bit.

"You could have tossed her in jail to sleep it off. She probably would have died in one of your cells."

"Thanks a lot." He thought for a moment. "Maybe I can help a little with your clinic's expenses."

"Like what?"

"You're with the public health service. Are you a board-certified medical examiner?"

"Yes."

"I need some help. I need an autopsy done on a body being kept at the funeral home. It will cost the county five hundred dollars if I ship the body down to Santa Fe for a coroner exam. If the coroner comes here, it will cost only three hundred dollars plus expenses. But I have to wait two weeks. That's two weeks of rental on the slab at the funeral home.

"Or I could have you do the autopsy. I'll pay you the same three-hundred-dollar fee. You can use it on the clinic if you want."

"I wouldn't be able to do any lab work here. You don't have the facilities."

"That's not a problem," Lansing coaxed. "Since this is probably a capital case, I can send all the samples down to the crime lab in Santa Fe."

"The clinic can use the money," Carerra admitted. "And since I'm in town already . . ." She looked at the sheriff. "How about this afternoon?"

"I'll have to make a few calls. Set things up. But I don't see why not."

"Just one thing, Lansing. I'm not a county official. I can sign the death certificate, but I'll need someone in there to witness the autopsy."

Lansing nodded. "I'll be in there with you."

"I guess I need to keep up my strength," Carerra said, reaching for a menu.

"Go ahead and charge it to my account." Lansing stood. "I'll start making the arrangements."

"Aren't you going to join me?"

"No." The sheriff shook his head. "Not if I'm going to watch an autopsy this afternoon."

Lansing stopped at the counter and explained to Kelly that Dr. Carerra's lunch would be on the county tab.

The doctor decided she needed to call the clinic at the reservation and tell them she would be in town for a while. She looked around the booth, then realized in her hurry to chew on Lansing she had left her purse in the truck. On her way past the counter she overheard Kelly and Velma comparing notes.

"What would you say, Kelly?" Velma asked, studying the sheriff as he strolled across the square toward the courthouse. "Forty, forty-two?"

"He's got to be at least that, 'cause he graduated the same year I started high school. Still in pretty good shape, though."

"Damned good shape," Velma leered. "He can park his boots under my bed anytime he wants."

"Yeah," the other waitress agreed. "Too bad he's still in love with his ex-wife."

Carerra pushed the diner door open and went outside.

# 7

"El Jadida, you're such a pretty horse," Bets McGaffrey said soothingly to her Arabian stallion as she combed the flanks. "Yes, you are." The magnificent Moroccan-bred horse nodded his head haughtily as if he understood his mistress's every word. Bets laughed. "You are conceited, aren't you?"

She reached into a saddlebag hanging over a stall gate and pulled out six sugar cubes. The horse ate the sweets eagerly when they were offered. She hugged the horse's neck.

"You know, you're getting old enough, Bets, you ought to be doing that with a male of your own species."

Bets released her stallion and turned to face Parker. The ranch foreman and her father's right-hand man leaned against the doorway to the stables. "That would leave you out, Parker."

Parker smiled. His smile looked more like a sneer. He was tall, thin, and mean. "You'll be, what, eighteen this year?"

Bets ignored him by returning to the chore of combing her horse. She shuddered at the thought of him standing there watching her. She wondered how long he *had* been there.

"Yeah, the years sure have gone by." Parker sauntered along the row of stables opposite El Jadida's. Parker avoided the stallion. "All those years off at boarding school . . . You sure did grow up."

"You wouldn't be talking like that if Mack McGaffrey were around!" she snapped.

"No, probably not. But he won't get back from Santa Fe till tonight. Then again, you won't tell him anything I said. You won't even talk to him. Your own father and you won't talk to him."

"That's none of your business." She began combing the horse even harder. El Jadida snorted in protest. "Sorry, boy." She patted him gently. "It's all right."

"You know, Elizabeth, you treat us all like trash around here. You might want to change your ways. One day you may need a friend." Bets continued to ignore him. "Just thought I'd let you know." Parker casually strolled out the doorway.

Once the foreman was gone, Bets could feel her stomach unknot. She put her face against the stallion. "You're my friend, aren't you, El Jadida." The horse whinnied soothingly. The tears welled in Bets's eyes. "Oh, Momma," the seventeen-year-old whispered, "I miss you."

# 8

WILLISTON ENTERED HIS ALBUQUERQUE STAFF OFFICES. When he was in Washington the office was manned by a single receptionist. When he was in New Mexico there were at least three additional staffers brought in from D.C., not counting Harding.

The four, usually unused, phone lines were tied up as aides tried to change Williston's schedule. They were making deals, making promises, making threats, all to accommodate the three-day vacation Williston announced for himself the night before. Only Harding had been told the truth. Williston was going out to find the Watcher and convince him to go along with the deal. The senator didn't want anything leaked about the deal possibly not going through. The cover story was, Williston was exhausted. He was taking three days off to recoup at Mack McGaffrey's ranch.

The three staffers hardly looked up as Williston strode through the reception area toward his private office. Harding was on the phone in the interior room. Williston signaled for him to hang up.

"Listen, George," Harding said into the phone, "the senator just walked in. Let me get back to you. . . . Good . . . Good-bye." Harding hung up the phone.

"Have you talked with Longtree yet?"

"No, Senator. He was filing depositions this morning. His secretary said he would call us as soon as he returned."

Williston took his seat behind his desk. He pressed the intercom. "Judy, bring me in a decaf."

"Yes, Senator." The response was perky. "I'll be right in."

"Are there any glitches yet?"

Harding looked at the notebook he was holding. "The chairman of the judiciary committee wasn't happy about you missing the confirmation hearing tomorrow."

"Screw 'em," Williston snorted. "Harper's a shoo-in anyway. . . . What else?"

"We made apologies to the Alexandria VFW. You were supposed to be their keynote speaker on Friday."

"Any day of the week they can step out their front door and trip over some retired general. They won't have trouble finding a replacement."

"Everything else we've rescheduled so far."

There was a short rap on the door before it opened. Judy stepped into the office carrying a coffee cup. "Your decaf, Senator." She set the cup in front of Williston.

The receptionist was a petite, bright, wholesome-looking coed-type with blond, pageboy-cropped hair. Harding had hired her. So far, from the rumors Williston had picked up, the chief of staff hadn't even been able to kiss her.

"Can I get you anything else?"

"No. I'm fine for now." Williston smiled at her. "Thanks."

Judy bounced out of the room. Williston took her for around twenty-five. Despite her bubbly innocence, the senator suspected she could suck out a man's tonsils in one kiss with very little effort.

Harding caught the senator watching Judy's exit.

"You hadn't planned on taking Mrs. Williston with you on this vacation, had you?"

"No." Williston didn't realize he had been caught staring. "She's taking a little trip of her own to visit family."

"You know, Senator, you might need to do some paperwork on this trip. Maybe you should take one of the staff along."

Williston looked at Harding. Harding made a slight motion with his head toward the door. "She worships you, Senator. I think she could make a very able assistant."

"Let me guess, Harding. You were a pimp in a previous life."

"Come on, Senator. That's the name of the game. You have power. Women are attracted to power. Enjoy it while you can."

"I'll pass. I'm married. *Happily* married."

The intercom buzzed.

"Yes," Williston responded.

"I have Mr. Longtree on the phone. You were expecting his call."

"Good. I'll take it." Williston pushed the speakerphone button. "Frank. Senator Williston."

"Good morning, Senator. My secretary said your office called."

"We did, indeed. I'd like to meet with the Watcher. I've rearranged my schedule and have the next few days free. Can you set up a meeting?"

"It's not an issue of setting up anything, Senator. There's no way to get in touch with him. It's simply a matter of showing up."

"I'm going to be at the McGaffrey ranch for three days, starting tonight."

"I know where that is."

"Good." Williston clapped his hands together. "You can meet me there for dinner this evening. We can talk about our plans over barbecue and take a run out to the strip in the morning."

Longtree hesitated before replying. "I'll have to do some rescheduling myself, but that can be arranged."

"Fine, Frank." Williston tried to sound jovial. "I'll see you there this evening." Williston disconnected the call before the lawyer could respond.

"I'm going home and packing," the senator said, heading for the door. "I'll be driving up to the ranch after lunch. As far as the press or anyone else is concerned, I'm incommunicado until you hear from me."

"No second thoughts about taking an assistant along?"

"I'm still a man, Harding. I'll have plenty of second thoughts, but I'm still going alone. See you in a few days."

# 9

San Phillipe was a sparsely populated county with a very meager tax base. It was almost impossible to keep a full-time physician. John Tanner was a general practitioner with one year left on a three-year contract. He ran the San Phillipe Community Clinic but his heart wasn't in it. He couldn't wait to get back to Philadelphia. He didn't like the outdoors. He didn't like New Mexico. He didn't like his salary. He resented being in Las Palmas and resented most of his patients.

"You know, Sheriff," Tanner confided to Lansing one night at the canteen not long after he had arrived, "I graduated from medical school with honors. I did my internship in one of the most prestigious hospitals on the East Coast. I had expectations of myself—"

"So what went wrong?" Lansing signaled the waitress for two more beers.

"I had to start paying off my education bills. I have no intention of being a G.P. the rest of my life. In fact, the only reason I'm here is to pay off some of my medical school debts. Eventually I'm going to do a residency in internal medicine. In the interim, though, I had hoped for a higher class of clientele."

"Getting too much veterinary work?" Lansing had seen him climb out of a horse trailer earlier that day.

Tanner nodded. "I didn't know *Evans on Bovine Diseases* would become my primary medical reference book."

"Your problem, Doctor, is that you need something to distract you from your work."

"I like golf," Tanner admitted. "But the only decent course is almost two hours away."

"I was thinking of something a little more immediate."

That night Lansing introduced Tanner to Velma.

Six months after the introduction, Marilyn asked the sheriff how the two were getting along.

"They're from different worlds. He's from the big city. She's from a small town. She loves country-and-western music. He likes the big bands from the forties. She likes the movies. He likes books. Dr. Tanner and Velma will never get married, if for no other reason than she will never leave Las Palmas and he will never stay in New Mexico. But they do have one mutual interest: sex. All through college and medical school, Tanner never had enough time for it. Velma's never had enough of it, period. It's a perfect match."

The long-term result of that introduction was Dr. Tanner would do Lansing any favor he requested.

The Las Palmas Clinic had a reception area, four examination rooms, and a small wing with a surgery. Tanner very seldom used the surgery. When the sheriff asked to use the surgery for performing an autopsy, Tanner was more than willing. In fact, he asked if he could attend. He said he could use a refresher course on human anatomy.

Duke Semple's body arrived from the funeral home at two P.M. To prevent deterioration and to keep the material from sticking to the epidermis, the body had been stripped of clothing when it was first placed on the refrigerated slab. The clothes were in a separate plastic bag. Other than that, the body was in the same condition as when Lansing had discovered it.

Drs. Carerra and Tanner stood over the body on the examination table with masks over their faces. Lansing stood to one side. On a table next to him was a cassette tape player/recorder equipped with a condenser microphone. All three wore surgical gowns.

"You can start recording, Sheriff." Dr. Carerra began her commentary as soon as she removed the sheet from the corpse. "I am examining a Caucasian male approximately fifty-five years of age. He is of normal height, approximately five foot nine to five foot ten inches. Weight at time of death: between one hundred and fifty-five to one hundred sixty-five pounds.

"He appears to have been normally developed with no external defects.

"Outward body appearance is normal.

"Feet and legs appear normal with no signs of trauma.

"Hands are normally developed. . . ." She stopped for a moment, examining the wrists more closely. "Wrists on both arms have chafing abrasions as if they had been tied by coarse rope."

She turned to Lansing. "Sheriff, was this individual tied up when you found him?"

"No," Lansing responded, stepping forward for a closer look.

Carerra pointed at one arm. There were definite chafing marks highlighted with dried blood. "He had to have been bound just prior to the time of death. The dried blood is smeared. Probably happened when the rope or strap was removed. What do you think, Doctor?"

Tanner examined the opposite wrist. "I would agree with that."

"Proceeding with the examination," Carerra continued. "There appear to be no other signs of distress to the upper extremities.

"Skull area shows no external signs of trauma. No contusions or lacerations on the face. . . . Correction, there is a small cut in the right corner of the mouth. If the subject had been bound, as indicated by the trauma to the wrists, the cut at the corner of the mouth would be consistent with being gagged at or around the same time.

"The neck appears normal.

"Proceeding to the upper abdomen, there are six identical puncture wounds in the area of the chest. The wounds are located between the upper sternum and the diaphragm. Each wound is approximately one centimeter across. From initial indications, the wounds were created by the use of a firearm at close range."

Lansing interrupted. "Why do you say 'close range'?"

"There are powder burns around each hole," Carerra explained. "We'll take samples to make sure. But if you look closely, the dried blood still has a hint of red to it. Also, the blood dripped straight down the chest because of gravity. The black from the powder is evenly distributed around each wound."

Lansing did look closer. He could see the powder burns around the holes. "How close did the gunman have to be?"

"I'm not a forensic specialist," the doctor admitted, "but I'd have to say no more than three or four feet away."

"That doesn't make sense." Lansing shook his head. "I found the weapon Beau used almost thirty feet away."

"Maybe Duke stumbled around for a few minutes before falling," Tanner observed.

Even though it had been smeared by the clothing,

the sheriff could see the blood had oozed from the wounds, down the chest to the stomach and waist area. The sheriff was puzzled.

"How long would it take for blood to drip like that?"

"Several minutes," Carerra admitted, "depending on how long the heart was still beating."

"When I found Duke, he was lying on his back. Wouldn't the blood have spread sideways across the chest?"

"Again, that would be consistent with him stumbling around first," Tanner noted.

"Yeah, I guess you're right. Let me just stay out of your hair."

With Dr. Tanner's assistance, Carerra continued with the autopsy. Lansing stood to the side keeping his mouth shut. When the dissection started, Lansing was glad he had skipped lunch. He had attended autopsies before, but he never enjoyed them. It was never the sight of a body being dismantled that affected him. It was the smell.

Carerra reached the first of the six slugs embedded in the body. "I've located a projectile in the upper lobe of the right lung. The puncture created by the projectile caused the lung to collapse, contributing to the death of the individual, although it was probably not the primary cause of death." She extracted the slug and held it up for closer examination. "The projectile has been removed. We'll send it to the crime lab for analysis, but it appears we are looking at a twenty-two or twenty-four caliber weapon."

"That can't be right, Doctor." The sheriff stepped forward again.

Carerra handed him the bullet. "I worked for three years in an emergency room in Albuquerque, Lansing. I've extracted everything from bird shot to a Winchester 458. I know my calibers. That's a twenty-two. Six millimeter tops."

Lansing studied the bullet. "The rifle Beau used was a thirty-thirty."

"That bullet did not come out of a thirty-thirty, Lansing. Either your man used a different gun or somebody else did the shooting."

"Well, just damn it all to hell." Lansing made the statement sound like a matter of fact.

"What's wrong?" Tanner asked.

"Looks like I have a real murder on my hands."

# 10

WILLISTON PULLED HIS LINCOLN TOWN CAR ALONG THE FIRST gas pump at the Phillips 66 station. There were only two islands with pumps. Nowhere was a sign reading "self-service."

The senator stepped out of the car as Ed Rodriguez ambled out of the station's bay. "Fill 'er up, mister?"

"Yeah," Williston said, stretching. He had been driving for two hours without a stop. "Any place around here to get a cup of coffee?" Williston was still wearing his suit, though the jacket was draped over the back of the passenger seat. He had loosened his tie and rolled up his shirtsleeves for comfort.

"Yes." Rodriguez smiled, removing the gas cap to the car. "The diner. About four blocks north. You can't miss it. It's right on Main Street."

"Do you happen to know how far it is to the McGaffrey ranch?"

The old man laughed. "You passed the south end of the ranch about five miles ago if you were coming from Los Alamos. You passed the north end of the ranch fifteen miles ago if you came in from Colorado."

"I'm driving in from Santa Fe. I want to know how far it is to the turnoff to the ranch house."

Rodriguez laughed again. "Then you still have another eight, ten miles to go. But you're in luck, because the diner's right on your way."

Williston paid for his gas and headed for the diner.

Three o'clock in the afternoon was the slowest time of the day for the Las Palmas Diner. The lunch crowd was gone. The dinner crowd wouldn't start showing up for two more hours. Even when school let out in the afternoon, the kids hung out at the Dixie Queen.

Williston had his choice of parking spots in front of the eatery. Except for the neon OPEN sign dangling in the window, he would have guessed the place was abandoned. Sliding out of his car, he decided to leave his suit jacket draped over the passenger seat. He did straighten his tie and roll his shirtsleeves down so he could button the cuffs. As he did, he noticed some activity behind the luncheon counter.

As Williston reached for the diner's door a hoarse whisper rasped: "Kelly! Kelly! Get out here!"

Williston entered the diner just when Kelly bellowed from the kitchen, "Speak up, Velma. I can't hear you."

The senator noticed the face of the waitress behind the counter turning a deep red as he approached. "Excuse me, miss, are you all right?" he asked.

"Yes," Velma choked. "Can I help you?"

"Do you have a washroom?"

"Certainly. Just go around the corner there. It's all the way to the back. It says 'men' on the door."

Williston smiled. "Thanks."

A few minutes later he emerged from the washroom. As he walked across the diner toward the counter he could hear one of the waitresses whisper, "Shh-shh-shh . . . Here he comes." He had a strong suspicion he had been the topic of their most recent conversation.

The two waitresses giggled to each other as Williston sat on one of the revolving stools at the counter. It was a moment before one of the women was composed enough to approach. She set a glass of water in front of the customer.

"Can I get you a menu?"

"No, thank you"—Williston leaned closer for a better look at the waitress's name tag—"Velma. Just a cup of decaf, please."

Velma hustled to the coffee machine to retrieve the orange-handled pot. A moment later she was filling the senator's cup.

"This your first time to Las Palmas?"

"I've been through here once or twice before. It's a nice little town."

"Thanks." Velma smiled. "We like it." She finished filling the cup. "Can I get you anything? Piece of pie?"

"No. Coffee's fine."

"Well, if you need anything, holler. I'll be right over there." Velma retreated to the far end of the counter, where Kelly was craning her neck to view the customer.

Williston suspected strangers were a novelty in Las Palmas. He did his best to mind his own business, but it was hard to ignore the two women behind the counter. They were neither subtle nor quiet. Their running conversation carried over the drone of the air conditioner and the noise of passing traffic.

"He is one good-looking man," Velma whispered.

Williston smiled to himself over the comment. He had quit thinking of himself as "good-looking" years earlier. He much preferred "distinguished." It added an air of respectability and wisdom.

"You know who he looks like?" Kelly asked in not very low tones. "Carter Williston."

"The senator?"

Kelly nodded.

"What would a U.S. senator be doing in Las Palmas?" Velma snorted.

"He was in Santa Fe yesterday. I saw it on TV. I'll bet he knows Merrill McGaffrey and he's on his way to the ranch."

"I still don't believe it."

From the corner of his eye, Williston watched as Kelly pushed her coworker toward the customer. "Why don't you go ask him."

"Why don't you?"

"Because he's your customer!"

Velma sounded reluctant. "Oh, all right." She picked the coffeepot from the machine and approached the senator. "More coffee?"

"No, thanks." Williston smiled at her again.

Velma started to leave. The senator could see Kelly point her finger at Velma, then at him.

Velma turned back to Williston. "Excuse me, but has anyone ever told you that you look like Senator Carter Williston?"

Williston did his best to keep a straight face. It wasn't often he went anywhere incognito. He decided he would have a little fun. He feigned a deep thought for a moment. "Come to think of it, I have been told that once or twice."

"I'll bet." Velma nodded. She seemed reluctant to end the conversation. "You up this way on business?"

"No, not really. I have a place down in Albuquerque. Thought I'd get out of town for a few days while my wife was visiting relatives."

"Oh, you're married." Velma sounded disappointed.

"Thirty-five years." Williston finished his coffee and stood. He pulled a five-dollar bill from his wallet and placed it on the counter. "That should cover the coffee. The rest is for you, miss. I enjoyed the visit." Williston headed for the door.

"Thank you, mister. Please, come back anytime."

The waitresses watched as the senator drove off.

"Well, what did he say?" Kelly pressed.

"He admitted people told him he looked like Senator Williston."

"What does he do?"

"I don't know." Velma sounded annoyed by all the questions. "He said he lived in Albuquerque and that he was taking a couple of days off."

"Wearing a suit?" Kelly snorted. "That was Senator Williston, I'll bet you."

"Then why didn't he say he was Senator Williston."

"Did you ask him?"

"No. Not directly."

"Girl, how many times do I have to tell you? If you want to get a straight answer out of somebody, you have to ask them a straight-out question."

Velma grabbed the five from the counter and rang up the bill on the register. "I still say, if that was Senator Williston, he would have said so."

Sheriff Lansing, Dr. Carerra, and Dr. Tanner entered the diner.

"Why, hello, John," Velma sang.

"Hi, Velma." Tanner took a seat at the counter. "How 'bout an orange juice?"

Lansing and Carerra ignored the courting ritual at the counter. The sheriff signaled the other waitress. "Kelly, a couple of coffees and I'll take a roast beef sandwich. You want anything to eat, Doctor?"

"No, thanks, Lansing." Carerra smiled. "I had lunch."

"We'll take them at the booth." The couple proceeded to the booth section along the far wall.

"What are you going to do now?" the doctor asked.

"I'll talk to the county attorney while Marilyn types the transcript from the autopsy. I don't know if he'll release Watson or not. Beau's still our only suspect."

"Don't you need motive and a weapon?"

"Those things would help. And we can't hold Beau forever without charging him with something."

Kelly approached the table with the coffee. "Sheriff, you'll never guess who was just in here."

"Who?" Lansing was distracted with other thoughts.

"Senator Carter Williston."

"What was he doing here?" Carerra asked.

"Having some coffee. Big as life. Sitting right over there where Dr. Tanner's sitting."

"Was there anyone with him?" Lansing was becoming interested.

"No. He was all by himself."

"Did he say he was Senator Williston?"

"No, but he was wearing an expensive suit and driving a brand-new Lincoln. He said he was taking a few days off. I told Velma he was probably going up to the McGaffrey ranch. Merrill McGaffrey always has important people visiting his ranch."

"They usually fly in," Lansing observed. "He has a private strip up there. Why would a senator drive there when he could have flown in? Besides, senators normally don't travel alone. They have assistants and secretaries hanging around so they don't have to do things for themselves. I think you have a case of mistaken identity."

"Oh." Kelly seemed deflated. She quickly changed the subject. "How'd it go with Duke Semple?"

Lansing shook his head. "Not well. He's still dead."

Kelly thought about the response a second, then burst out laughing. She playfully slapped Lansing on the arm. "Oh, Sheriff, you're such a kidder. . . . I'll go get your sandwich."

When Kelly was out of the way, Carerra asked, "You don't want anyone to know the results of the autopsy?"

"Not yet. If someone else did kill Duke, I don't want them to know we're looking for them. I'll have Stu

Ortega run the samples down to the crime lab in Santa Fe tomorrow. Maybe ballistics can tell us what kind of gun we're looking for.

"While he's doing that, I'll take a trip to the foothills. If someone else was up there, some of Beau's story would start making sense. He said they had removed six boxes of pottery from an ancient Indian village. I found some pottery shards, but no complete vessels like he was talking about."

"Disturbing ancient sites like that is against federal law."

Lansing nodded. "Why do you think they were up there in the middle of the night? Somebody else might have had the same idea and jumped them. Whoever jumped them could have killed Duke and taken the pottery."

"When I was having lunch, one of the waitresses mentioned that Beau said he was chased by monsters or demons. Something like that."

"He was drunk when we picked him up. I blew off most of what he said. I was sure once he sobered up he would change his story."

"Did he?"

"Not one bit. But part of his story checked out. He said something came after him and he shot it. His rifle was empty and Duke was dead. The rest I attributed to the booze, or him trying to cover up the fact that he shot Duke, or both. I need to go back and take a closer look."

"Is there anything I can do to help?"

Lansing gave her a funny look. "Why, Doctor? You've done more than enough."

"I don't know." She looked a little embarrassed. "I thought a lot about what you did for the Akees. I know how the Indians from the reservation get treated at some of the other towns around here. If the Akees had gone to McPherson, the police would have thrown Susan into jail to sleep it off and she'd be dead right now. You at least try to show them respect."

"They deserve 'at least' that."

"I need to get back to the reservation." Carerra stood.

Lansing stood also. "I need to see about getting you that three hundred dollars."

"I have to be in town tomorrow. I have supplies coming in by bus. If you could leave a check with Marilyn, I'll pick it up from her."

"Who should the check be made out to?"

"The reservation clinic. They need the money more than I do."

On her way out, Dr. Carerra stopped at the counter to thank Tanner for his help. Lansing sat and watched her glide across the floor and out the door.

"Velma would give a week's wages for you to look at her like that." Kelly placed the roast beef sandwich in front of Cliff.

Lansing was a little startled to find the waitress next to him. "I don't know what you're talking about."

"The unfortunate thing is, Sheriff, you probably don't."

Lansing stood. "Wrap that to go for me, Kelly. I'll eat it at the office."

"Whatever you want, Sheriff." Kelly picked up the sandwich and headed back to the kitchen.

Lansing watched the light green pickup truck back into the street, then drive away. He wondered if his face did betray his feelings. Then he had to stop and consider what his feelings really were. He was grateful when Kelly returned with his lunch, rescuing him from his self-analysis. He paid for the sandwich and coffees, then headed for his office.

# 11

SENATOR WILLISTON WHEELED HIS TOWN CAR ONTO THE paved road that led from the main highway to the ranch house complex. The complex was not visible from Route 15. Knots of cattle ranged casually on either side of the private road. Wherever possible they huddled under scrub piñon trees to escape the direct sun.

The road eventually rounded a low hill. In the valley below was the McGaffrey ranch: a series of barns, outbuildings, stables, bunkhouses, guest houses, plus the main house. One-hundred-year-old cottonwood trees shaded much of the grounds. Corralled pastureland, greened by an elaborate sprinkler system, contrasted sharply with the sun-baked red and tan landscape that surrounded the ranch. Along one side of the arrangement was a small stream. The stream ran all year, fed by the melting snows of the mountains to the west. Williston couldn't help but be impressed by the serene splendor of the layout.

As he maneuvered down the hill a movement caught his attention from the corner of his eye. He turned to find a young woman on a beautiful Arabian horse racing him for the one-lane bridge that crossed the stream. He checked his speedometer. He was going thirty-five miles an hour. His first instinct was to slow down. Instead he pressed on the accelerator, goaded by an immature desire to compete and win.

The Town Car surged ahead of the horse. In response, the rider spurred her horse. In a matter of seconds the stallion and car were even.

Williston watched the horse at full gallop. It was magnificent. He kept an eye on the rapidly approaching bridge. He didn't want anything stupid to happen. He told himself he would slow down in plenty of time to let the horse go ahead. The streambed was five feet below the bridge and at least twenty feet across. He knew his car couldn't negotiate the crossing without the bridge, nor could the horse.

That's when he saw the truck. It pulled around one of the barns tugging a double-wide horse trailer. The two men inside the truck seemed oblivious of the approaching Lincoln.

From the way the rear tires were kicking up dust, Williston realized the driver was gunning his engine, intent on beating the Town Car to the bridge. The senator hit his brakes. The stallion sped past him. The Town Car skidded to a stop on the meager shoulder.

Williston threw open the door and started yelling at the rider to stop.

The truck kept coming. The horse never slowed. Williston estimated the collision would occur on his side of the bridge.

The rider looked up to see the approaching vehicle. Instead of reining in her horse, she spurred it even harder. Williston couldn't help but wonder at the suicide he was about to witness.

The truck was now on the bridge. There didn't seem to be an escape for the horse or its master. Then with one mighty kick, the horse leapt across the tiny chasm. Williston's view of the effort was partially blocked by the truck and trailer.

Both the driver and passenger whooped like idiots as they sped past Williston. "You asshole!" Williston bellowed after the truck.

He turned back to the stream, expecting the worst. Instead, the young rider sat safely on the back of her dancing steed on the opposite bank. She waved at Williston.

Shaken, the senator got back into his car and continued toward the ranch house.

Holding the reins to her horse, Bets greeted the visitor as he climbed from his car. "You must be Senator Williston."

"Yes, young lady, I am. And I don't mind saying you scared the ever-living daylights out of me."

Bets laughed. "You mean jumping the streambed. We do that all the time." She patted her stallion affectionately. "What do you think of El Jadida?"

"He's a magnificent animal." Williston reached up and caressed the horse gently along the neck.

"I'm surprised he let you do that. He doesn't take well to strangers."

"He must know I like horses." The senator smiled.

"You ride a lot?"

"Not in many years," Williston admitted. "Not since I was about your age."

"I'm forgetting my manners." Bets removed the leather riding glove she was wearing and extended her hand. "I'm Elizabeth McGaffrey. We met a few years back."

Williston shook hands with her. "Quite a few years back. That was during my campaign." He laughed. "You were just a little girl then."

"She has grown up, hasn't she?"

The two turned to find Bets's father approaching from the main house.

"Hell of a horse too." McGaffrey slapped the horse on the rear. El Jadida skittered nervously as Bets calmed him down. Williston caught the hateful look Bets gave her father. "Paid thirty-five thousand for him at an auction in Morocco. He's named after the town he comes from. Good to see you could make it, Carter." The handshake between the two men was brief and formal.

"I think you should know a couple of your boys ran me off the road back there and nearly killed your daughter."

McGaffrey laughed. "Those boys were just having some fun. They've been out mending fences for two weeks. They've got some money in their pockets and they're out to have a good time. I saw the whole thing from the house. They gave you a wide berth and Bets here can take care of herself."

It appeared to Williston that that was the end of the matter.

"You should have let me fly you up, Carter."

"I enjoyed the drive. Gave me a chance to unwind."

"Come on up to the house. Let me get you a drink."

"I'm ready for one. Let me grab my things." Williston started toward his trunk.

"Forget it," McGaffrey ordered. "One of the boys will bring your stuff in." McGaffrey started toward the house.

Williston turned to Bets. "You coming with us?"

"No," Bets replied flatly. "I need to take care of El Jadida. I'll be up later."

Williston watched as she led her horse away.

"Coming, Carter?" McGaffrey called to his guest.

"Yeah." Williston followed his host into the house.

The "den" was half the size of a basketball court. The ceiling was vaulted with rough-hewn exposed beams. The leather upholstered furniture blended comfortably with the three white adobe walls. The fourth wall was built of stone with a fireplace tall enough for a man to stand in erect. The decor was strictly "southwestern," with Indian blankets, pottery, and artifacts underscoring the atmosphere.

McGaffrey handed Williston a Scotch on the rocks. "My only complaint, Carter, is that I don't get to spend enough time around here. I'm either down in Santa Fe or Albuquerque running my businesses or overseas making deals." He plopped down in a chair with a bourbon. "Take a load off."

"I've been sitting all afternoon." Williston took a sip of his drink. "If it's all the same, I think I'll stand for a while."

"Suit yourself."

Williston casually studied the Indian artwork in the room.

"What do you know about this Longtree character?" McGaffrey asked.

"Not much," Williston allowed. "He's the legal representative for the Zuni tribe. He has offices in Santa Fe. Seems to be conscientious enough."

"He's half Zuni, half Navajo," the millionaire expounded. "His parents met at college down at New Mexico State. He grew up Navajo, but he evidently has close ties to both tribes."

Williston raised his glass as a toast. "You've been doing your homework."

"My lawyers have. Helps to know where the other side is coming from when you're negotiating. You need to know their strengths and their weaknesses. That way you can avoid what the opposition is good at and concentrate on their weak areas."

"I thought the negotiations were over. The agreement is essentially ironed out."

"The negotiations aren't over till the deed's filed at the courthouse." McGaffrey got angry as he spoke. "You still have some old Indian running around the hills trying to claim ancestral privilege. Meanwhile there are seven thousand Zunis two hundred miles away who can't make a decision without his okay. Tell me that makes sense, Senator. Tell me with a straight face everything is 'essentially ironed out.'" He downed his entire drink in a single gulp.

"Mack, I'll meet with the man tomorrow. If he's as wise as Longtree claims he is, there's not going to be a problem."

McGaffrey went to the bar and fixed himself another drink. "You don't have any guarantees, though. Do you?"

"No," the senator admitted.

"I'm not a gambler, Williston. You won't find me traipsing off to Vegas to throw my money away. I like sure things. But if something does look like it might be a gamble, I'll hedge my bet."

"How?"

"You're going to talk to this old Indian tomorrow. I'm not going to roll over if he says 'no.' We still have this lawyer, Longtree. He's not stupid. You don't see him living out on the reservation in absolute squalor. He's handled cases for the Zuni and the Navajo. He'd like to build a practice that represents all the Indian nations of the Southwest. That takes money . . . and every man has his price."

Williston studied his glass for a moment. "Why are you so hot on making this deal happen?"

McGaffrey took a swallow from his second drink. "Let's just say I'm a good American and a savvy businessman who hates to see good land go to waste."

"With the land swap, the Anasazi Strip will belong to the federal government. What's your take out of all this?"

"I don't know that it really concerns you, Carter. You pull this off, I'll support you for reelection next year. That's all you need to know and probably care about." McGaffrey finished his drink. "Help yourself to another Scotch. Ring the bell by the door when you want to see your room. Ramón will take you back. We'll be eating around six." McGaffrey started for the door.

"Where are you going?" Williston interrupted.

"I have work to do." McGaffrey left with no other formalities.

Williston pondered his drink and his options. A phone sat on one of the end tables. He thought for a moment, then picked up the receiver. Using his phone card, a second later he was talking to Harding.

"Yeah, I made it here just fine. Listen, I want you to find out if McGaffrey or one of his front companies has been talking to the Bureau of Land Management. . . . I don't know what about. That's what I want you to find out. . . . I know you'll have to do an end run around the secretary of the interior. . . . And that's another thing. The secretary's office rolled over too easily on this land swap. Find out what kind of link Milton has with McGaffrey. There's got to be something. . . . No, that's all. See you in a few days."

Williston hung up the phone. Looking at his glass, he realized the ice had melted. As he walked across the room to freshen the drink, he failed to notice the hallway door closing quietly behind him.

##  12

THE LATE AFTERNOON HAD COOLED TO THE POINT THAT McGaffrey chose to have dinner served on the patio. Longtree had arrived at five-thirty, which gave him time to change before cocktails. The dinner party was small: McGaffrey, his man Parker, Longtree, Williston, and Bets. The young lady remained aloof, only involving herself in the conversation when she was asked a direct question. Even then her response would amount to a simple "yes," "no," or a shrug of her shoulders.

McGaffrey and Parker seemed oblivious of her attitude. Williston wondered if he was so out of touch with the younger generation that surly behavior was the norm. Then he reminded himself of how cheerful she had been after the race for the bridge. Her behavior had changed abruptly when McGaffrey first approached. It hadn't changed since then.

McGaffrey motioned everyone to take their seats. As they settled into their chairs, the host turned to Longtree. "You keep referring to this individual called the Watcher. Does he go by anything else?"

"The literal translation of his name from the Zuni is 'the Father Who Walks on the Wind.' He has taken the Anglicized name Joseph Windwalker. Or just Windwalker."

"I see," McGaffrey commented. "That's interesting." He fell silent as the cook set plates of salad and steak in front of the guests.

"Now, you say this Windwalker lives out on Anasazi Strip?" the host asked once everyone had been served.

"Yes," Longtree replied, cutting a slice of steak.

"There's a lot of acreage out there," McGaffrey continued. "I suppose you know where to look for him."

"Yes. It's not difficult if he wants you to find him." Longtree took a taste of the steak. "This is delicious, Mr. McGaffrey. My compliments to your cook."

"Ramón will be pleased you liked it." McGaffrey looked at his daughter. The food on her plate was untouched. "What's the matter, Bets? You're not eating."

"I guess I'm not hungry."

"Well, then, why don't you just run along. Ramón can whip you up something if you get hungry later."

Betsy stood. "Senator Williston, Mr. Longtree. If you'll excuse me."

Williston and Longtree stood at the same time. "Certainly, Elizabeth," the senator replied. Once Bets was gone, Longtree complimented his host on having such a beautiful daughter.

"Yes," McGaffrey agreed. "She takes after her mother."

The conversation at the dinner table became animated. Of the four men present, three had their own area of expertise and the ability to tell a good story. McGaffrey was a businessman who enjoyed talking about how he could beat out the competition. Williston discussed politics and the different personalities in Washington. Longtree talked about the legal system with all its inanity and corruption.

Parker said nothing. Williston had an uneasy feeling the foreman's silence was not because he couldn't contribute to the conversation. It seemed more that he was weighing their words, studying their attitudes and mannerisms. Studying their strengths and weaknesses was the way McGaffrey had put it. Williston concentrated on the story the lawyer was telling, forgetting about his concerns.

When the table was cleared away, McGaffrey suggested they move to the den for cigars and brandy. Although Williston was not a smoker, he did enjoy the occasional cigar. McGaffrey stocked only the best.

After lighting his cigar, Longtree studied the artifacts and artwork displayed in the room. Six Indian blankets adorned the walls in different places. The lawyer pointed at each, one at a time, announcing its origin: "Zuni, Navajo, Pueblo, Hopi, Apache, Arapaho."

"I'm very impressed, Mr. Longtree," McGaffrey lauded his accomplishment. "I would expect a man to recognize symbols from his own tribe and maybe one or two others. You got all six correct."

"No. You are the one to be complimented, Mr. McGaffrey," Longtree corrected. "Few white men find it necessary to distinguish between the different nations. We're thought of as one homogeneous group of people. We're not. . . . I understand your Museum of the Americas goes out of its way to make that distinction."

"It's not my museum, Mr. Longtree. I had a small part in making it happen. That's all."

"From the press releases, I got the impression you donated hundreds of artifacts and pieces of art to be on permanent display."

"That may be true"—McGaffrey tried to sound modest—"but a private collection doesn't mean much if it can't be appreciated by more than a handful of people."

"Do you mind my asking how much the blankets cost?"

"Oh . . ." McGaffrey thought for a moment. "Anywhere from three hundred to five hundred dollars."

"How much profit do you make when you sell blankets like these to dealers overseas?" Longtree made the question sound casual.

"That, counselor, is none of your damned business." McGaffrey kept the tone of his voice light and friendly.

"I was just curious," Longtree said, taking a sip of brandy. He pointed at the Navajo sample. "A friend of mine was in Paris this past year. He saw a blanket almost identical to this one going for six thousand dollars."

"Well, you know how those French are," McGaffrey said with a laugh. "What a dealer charges in Europe is hardly an indictment of my business practices."

"No, but I am tired of businessmen taking advantage of Native Americans. It may take a year to loom one of those blankets. You or one of your representatives show up at the trading post and pay dirt for someone else's hard work, then turn around and make a huge profit."

"That's simply being an entrepreneur. It's all legal and aboveboard."

"But is it fair, Mr. McGaffrey?" He turned to Williston. "Do you think it's fair, Senator?"

"I don't think the Native Americans have gotten a fair shake on a lot of things, Frank. But as a legislator I'm not going to interfere with a free-market economy. If a Navajo craftsman can get a better price for his work somewhere else, let him. There's nothing that says he has to sell to Mr. McGaffrey."

Longtree picked up a small vase from a table. "I suppose you're right, Senator." He studied the vase closely, then looked at McGaffrey.

"Mayan," McGaffrey explained. "Pre-Columbian. I estimate the value of that piece you're holding at about five thousand dollars. It's from a dig I sponsored six or seven years ago. A site just south of Mérida on the Yucatán.

"I have a respectable collection: Aztec, Mayan, Incan, Anasazi. . . ." McGaffrey noticed Williston studying a round stone tablet on the mantel. "The piece you're looking at, Senator, is Aztec."

"One of their calendars?" Williston guessed.

"Not exactly," their host explained. "It depicts the life cycle of a man. The ancients found certain numbers to contain mystical qualities. For the Aztecs the numbers four and thirteen were held in high esteem. Their calendar was built on a four-year cycle, just the way our leap year comes every four years. And the Aztecs thought the normal life span of a man was thirteen four-year cycles, or fifty-two years. Back then, that was probably right. I think that concept came from cultures older than theirs, though.

"Like the Romans, the Aztecs were conquerors and assimilators. They originated very little and were historical latecomers. They didn't even show up in what is now Mexico City until A.D. 1325."

"You do know your Native American history," Williston commented. "But . . . how do you come by all these artifacts?"

"Expeditions I've sponsored. I'm a firm believer in following legends and myths. In the eighteen hundreds Schliemann found Troy using the *Iliad* as his road map. I've found the same success using Native American lore. I've acquired a few pieces from auctions. I am a well-known collector. Sometimes I'll get a call from another collector who has an item they've decided to part with."

"You know it's against federal law to remove relics from public lands," Longtree pointed out.

"It's also illegal to remove relics from Indian lands," McGaffrey countered, "but that doesn't stop your fellow tribesmen from raping historical sites for a quick buck.

"There are sellers and there are buyers. I'm a buyer,

if the right thing is being sold. And there's nothing in the law that says I have to ask where it came from."

"I'm not a lawyer," Williston observed, "but I think you're walking a very fine line on that one, Mack."

McGaffrey laughed. "You're probably right, Senator." He turned to Longtree. "But you know what, counselor? You have given me a thought. I have done quite well financially because of the industry and talent of Native Americans. Maybe there's an opportunity for me to pay some of that back. I have contacts with all the major galleries in Europe. Instead of me being the middleman and making all the profits, why don't I just be the conduit? A direct link between your craftsmen and the retailers."

Longtree considered the proposition for a moment, then smiled. "I like that. We could set up a cooperative between the different tribes. The cooperative could be a single-source supplier. We could set our own rates."

"Now you're talking like a true capitalist, counselor." He turned back to Williston. "At the risk of sounding rude, Senator, I think Mr. Longtree and I will step aside for a while and discuss this business venture."

"You don't need to do that." Williston set his glass on the bar. "It's getting late. I think I'll take a little walk outside, then turn in."

As he left the room, Williston thought about McGaffrey's philosophy: find out your opponent's strengths and weaknesses. Longtree let his greatest weakness show right up front. He did not like the way white men like McGaffrey took advantage of Native Americans financially. McGaffrey was through the door before Longtree knew he had opened it. They were business partners now. Williston wondered how long it would take McGaffrey to find Longtree's price.

The night air was cool and crisp as the senator strolled along the corral leading to the stables. He supposed he was drawn there by the lit interior. He looked inside. Bets was currying El Jadida one last time before putting the stallion into the stall for the night.

"Ever get anything to eat?"

Bets jumped at the sound of the voice. "Oh, Senator! You scared me."

Williston laughed. "Sorry. Didn't mean to, though I guess I'm even for this afternoon."

Bets laughed. It was the first time Williston had seen her smile since their first meeting. He walked up and gently caressed the horse. "He really is a beautiful horse. You take good care of him."

"When I'm here," Bets said with a sigh. "Summers and holidays. The rest of the time I'm off at school." She continued brushing her horse. "I'm going to college this fall. I wanted to go to the University of New Mexico, but my father has me all set up for some snobby school in the East. Just as well, I suppose. The farther away from him, the better."

They were bitter words, but Williston found them delivered rather flatly, as a matter of course. "You and your father don't get along?"

"Not very well. In fact, not at all."

"Do you mind my asking why?"

"Yes, I do!" The tone of her response told Williston to back off. "I'm sorry," she apologized. "I shouldn't have snapped at you."

"That's okay. I was poking my nose in places it didn't belong."

Bets softened her tone. "How long have you known my father?"

The senator shrugged. "I don't know. Fifteen years, maybe."

"Did you know my mother?"

"No, not really. I met her at a cocktail party at the

White House. She was a very striking woman. It must have been awfully hard on you when she . . ." Williston caught himself before finishing the sentence. "When she died."

"You mean when she committed suicide," Bets corrected. "I'm a big girl. I know all about stuff like that."

"I'm sorry."

"You shouldn't be. It wasn't your fault." Bets smiled a mirthless smile. "Isn't it funny? People go around all the time apologizing for things they had nothing to do with. And the people who should be apologizing spend all their time explaining why something wasn't their fault."

"That's an astute observation, Elizabeth. Unfortunately, that's also the way of the world."

"Then the world sucks!" Bets set down her brush and led El Jadida into his stall. She removed his halter and bit, then closed the stall gate. "Senator, if you don't mind, I'd feel a lot more comfortable if you called me Bets. That's what my friends call me."

Williston smiled. "I'd be honored to call you Bets."

The senator had one great regret in his life—there had been no children in his marriage. It wasn't for lack of trying. Karen had gotten pregnant three times but had miscarried on each one. The third attempt nearly killed her. They had to give up their dreams of birthday parties, ballet lessons, and graduation gifts. It was a private pain he and Karen shared. No one was to blame. It was simply the way God had planned things. Still, Williston couldn't help but wonder, if he and his wife had had a daughter, would she have been like Bets? He hoped so.

The two walked back to the main house together talking about more pleasant things.

# 13

LANSING SAT AT HIS DESK TRYING TO TYPE THE ANALYSIS REquest forms for the autopsy samples. He had let Marilyn go at five-thirty. Wednesday night was church night. The half-eaten roast beef sandwich sat at the corner of his desk. The buzzer rang on his intercom.

"Yes?" the sheriff asked, distracted by his task at hand.

"I have a call for you, Sheriff. Line one."

Lansing was puzzled. "Larry? Are you on already?" Larry Peters was the night deputy. His shift ran from ten P.M. until seven A.M.

"Yes, sir. It's eleven o'clock."

*Damn!* Lansing thought. Aloud he said, "Thanks," and pressed the button for line one. "Sheriff Lansing."

"Sheriff, this is Margarite Carerra."

The *Margarite* threw him off. It quickly dawned on him to whom he was talking. "Oh, Dr. Carerra. What can I do for you?"

"I'm sorry to call so late. . . . I just wanted to let you know I talked to the hospital in Farmington a few minutes ago. Susan Akee is going to be fine."

"That's great. I'm glad to hear that." He felt awkward, not sure what he was supposed to say next. "Anything else?"

"No . . ." the doctor responded slowly. "I guess not." She was quiet for a moment, then: "Oh, are you still going out tomorrow?"

"Yes, I had planned on it. In fact, I need to throw some things together tonight before I head out."

"I was just curious if you knew what time you'd be getting back."

Lansing thought for a moment. "Late afternoon, maybe. Is there something I could help you with?"

"Well, no," said Carerra. "I just thought I could delay my trip into town tomorrow till later in the day. If you were around I thought we could get together for a cup of coffee or something."

"Okay." He tried to sound casual. "Why don't we meet at the diner, say, five o'clock."

"Five o'clock would be fine." Again there was an awkward silence. "Well, then," the doctor concluded, "I guess I'll see you then. Good night, Lansing."

"Good night, Doctor." Lansing hung up the phone.

He concentrated on finishing the request forms, but his thoughts kept drifting back to the telephone conversation. It had been a long time since he had gone out with a woman, not that the opportunity hadn't come up before. He hadn't been interested.

Lansing signed the typed forms, then went to his evidence cabinet. He put the bullets, shells, fingerprint samples, and other items for the crime lab into a cardboard box. He looked at his inventory list. Everything that was on the sheet was in the box. He couldn't help thinking there was something missing, but each item cross-checked. He shrugged it off as he set the box on his desk. There were other things on his mind—chief among them, Margarite Carerra.

# 14

THE SENATOR AND THE LAWYER HAD ARRANGED FOR AN EARLY start. Longtree guessed the drive from the ranch would take an hour to an hour and a half. After that, he wasn't sure how much farther it would be.

"Just what does that mean?" Williston had asked warily the evening before.

"We may have to do some hiking . . . or possibly horseback riding. It will depend on what kind of arrangements have been made."

"Arrangements by who?" McGaffrey had asked.

"The Watcher. He has his own way of doing things," Longtree explained. "But just in case, Senator, I'd wear a comfortable pair of shoes."

Activity started early at the ranch. When Williston and Longtree arrived for breakfast, McGaffrey, Bets, and Parker were already eating on the patio. Williston wore khaki pants, a white Western-style shirt, and riding boots. Longtree was in denim jeans and a light cotton plaid shirt. His boots were well worn. Both carried their Stetsons as they emerged from the house.

"Good morning," McGaffrey greeted them cheerfully.

Parker said nothing.

"Thought you two city slickers were going to get an early start." the host joked.

"It's only six-thirty," Williston protested. "I think I'm doing remarkably well. I'm usually sleeping at this time."

"Same here," the lawyer agreed, stifling a yawn.

Williston sat next to Bets. "Good morning, Bets."

The young lady put her best effort into a smile. "Good morning, Senator."

"I'm glad to see you're at least eating today." He tried to sound upbeat. She continued her plastic smile, but only nodded.

As the guests settled down to the coffee and juice on the table, Ramón took their omelette orders.

Williston noticed the single pot of coffee. "I don't suppose you have decaffeinated?" he asked.

"No, señor," Ramón apologized. "Would you prefer tea?"

Parker snickered at the question.

"That's all right," Williston said, adding cream to his cup. "This will be fine." He ignored the foreman. "What's on your agenda today, young lady?"

"Riding." She didn't elaborate.

"I was looking at that Jeep of yours, counselor," McGaffrey commented, finishing off the last of his eggs. "Looks like you do some pretty hard driving in that thing."

Longtree nodded. "I have two cars. I have a nice Buick I use for in town when I go to court. But most of my clients live out on the reservations. They don't care what kind of car I drive. Just as long as I can get to them."

"Do you think it's going to make it today?"

"I'm not worried. It may look a little worn on the outside, but the engine's as good as new."

"What time can I expect you back this way?" McGaffrey asked.

"Late afternoon," the lawyer guessed. "I have to be back in Santa Fe tonight."

"If it would help, I could send Parker along in another Jeep. He could bring the senator back here and you could head on down to Santa Fe after your meeting."

Longtree declined the offer. "Thanks, but I don't think the Watcher would appreciate an uninvited guest. He's very leery of strangers."

"Just a suggestion." McGaffrey shrugged.

Ramón brought out two plates of steaming omelettes, setting them in front of the guests.

Williston took a whiff of his plate. "Smells delicious."

"Thank you, señor." Ramón retrieved McGaffrey's and Parker's empty plates and headed back to the kitchen.

"Excuse us a minute," McGaffrey said, standing. "Ranch business."

He signaled Parker to follow and the two men went inside the house.

"Senator, if you don't mind." Bets stood. "I wanted to be out with El Jadida by now."

"Certainly." Williston stood when the young lady left.

The guests sat quietly enjoying their meals. It was almost ten minutes before McGaffrey returned carrying a fresh cup of coffee. "Where's Bets?"

"She was anxious to go riding," the senator commented, still enjoying his meal.

"That girl." McGaffrey shook his head. "Ramón is fixing sandwiches for you. It might be a long day. He'll also have a jug of water. I told him to put everything in your Jeep."

"That was very thoughtful, Mr. McGaffrey," Longtree responded between bites.

McGaffrey waited until the lawyer finished his

breakfast before he asked, "Have you given any more thought to my proposal from last night, counselor?"

"Yes, Mr. McGaffrey, I have," Longtree replied, wiping his face with a cloth napkin. "I would like to ask for a continuance. I need to research the proposal a little more before I commit myself."

"I wouldn't hesitate too long, Mr. Longtree. My proposition could be overcome by events, in which case the offer would be withdrawn."

Williston watched the lawyer's face. The muscles in the counselor's jaw tightened as he pondered the situation. The senator couldn't help but wonder what Longtree's price was.

"I'll have a firm answer for you this afternoon, Mr. McGaffrey. That's the best I can do."

"Fine," the millionaire replied calmly. "If that's the best you can do. Let's hope this afternoon isn't too late."

Williston was aching to know what the cryptic conversation meant. He knew asking McGaffrey was out of the question. There was a chance he could get Longtree to open up on the drive to the Strip. "Well, Frank," the senator interrupted as he finished the last of his omelette, "I suppose we need to get rolling." He stood. "Thanks for the hospitality, Mack. We'll see you sometime this afternoon."

"Yes," Longtree echoed. "Thanks for everything."

The two men put on their hats and headed for the Jeep.

Longtree turned south on Highway 15 toward Las Palmas.

"Have you ever been near the Anasazi Strip, Senator?"

Williston shook his head. "No. Not that I recall."

"The Anasazi Strip is pretty much an ill-defined piece of territory, despite what your environmental study claims," the attorney explained. "It sits on the eastern boundary of San Phillipe County, but a lot of it spills into the western part of Dwyer County. The Bureau of Land Management claims the total area covers over two hundred square miles."

Williston quoted the text of the impact study: "Two hundred and fifty-seven, to be exact."

"They're still guessing," Longtree insisted. "They don't really know because the area hasn't been surveyed. Oh, they've tried to survey the boundaries. If you look at a BLM chart, the entire area is sectioned off. But they don't know what's in the sections."

"Why not?"

The lawyer shrugged. "Lack of interest. Lack of money. It's tough country to get around in. There are no roads. Maybe a few trails. It's mostly steep hills and blind canyons."

"Why is the Zuni nation so reluctant to give it up? They settled on a reservation almost two hundred miles away."

"They didn't settle there. They were *settled* there . . . by the white man. There's a big distinction between the two, Senator.

"You have to understand the Zuni heritage. We are descended from the Anasazi, the first great civilization in North America.

"You can argue about dates, and the Mayan Empire on the Yucatán—but north of the Rio Grande River the Anasazi had the first great culture. They were not hunter-gatherers like the Plains Indians. They were sedentary. They farmed the land with elaborate irrigation systems. They built cities.

"Before a youth could pass on to manhood he had to recite his lineage. Kind of like the 'begat's in Genesis. But I'm not talking about needing to know a few dozen names. They had to know four and five hundred ancestors. It could take the youth two hours to recite the entire list. They traced their families back ten thousand years . . . to the beginning of time as they knew it . . . to the time of the creation."

"If they were so civilized, what happened to them?"

"It depends on which theory you subscribe to. The popular belief is that there were dramatic climate changes: the crops dried up; the people moved on. There are others who think they were conquered by the Aztecs and forced into slavery. The Aztec civilization emerged about the same time the Anasazi disappeared. And there are a lot of elements in Aztec religion and mythology that resemble ancient Zuni beliefs."

"Which one do you believe?"

"I'm not a historian, Senator. I'm a pragmatist."

"I still don't understand the reluctance of your people to relinquish claims on the Anasazi Strip. They could have made similar claims on Mesa Verde National Park, but they didn't. I mean, there are Anasazi sites from Texas to California. What's so important about this one piece of land?"

"What is so important about Israel to the Jews? It is their birthright. It is their heritage. It is a mysticism that binds a people together. I can't explain it any better than that."

"But you think the land trade is a good deal for the Zuni people."

"Yes," Longtree admitted, slowing his Jeep as they entered the Las Palmas city limits. "But then, I don't believe in the old gods like some of my people still do. I don't believe I'll offend any spirits. I don't think one piece of land could be any more consecrated than the next."

Williston watched the diner as they passed. It was still breakfast time. He was surprised to see the parking area filled with cars and trucks. His first impression of the eatery was that no one ever ate there. He smiled to himself about the encounter with the waitress the day before and thought he might stop there the next day and tell her she was right.

# 15

LANSING SAT IN THE DINER HAVING BREAKFAST. ACROSS THE table from him were Stu Ortega and Joe Cortez, his two daytime deputies. Velma hovered around the tables making sure all the coffee cups stayed full, insurance against a poor tip.

"Now, Stu," the sheriff ordered between bites, "I don't want you hanging around in Santa Fe all day. Take the bullets, rifle, and fingerprint samples to the Highway Patrol Crime Lab. The tissue samples and autopsy report go to the Santa Fe County Coroner's Office. You don't have to wait for anything. They can fax us the results."

"Don't worry. I'll drop the stuff off and come right back."

"Yeah," the sheriff said doubtfully. Stu Ortega was a likable enough guy; Lansing just couldn't depend on him. "And another thing. Would you please clean out your patrol car again. You've got so much crap stuffed in the backseat you're starting to look like a garbage truck."

"Don't worry, Chief. I'll get it. I promise."

Lansing turned to his other deputy. "Joe, since the radio's out in your car, I'll leave my Jeep for you. You'll have patrol today. I'll haul Cement Head up to the hills with me in my truck. I should be back before five. If I'm not, don't worry. I don't go up in hill country without provisions. Any questions?"

Joe raised his hand. "What if the county attorney says to let Beau Watson out?"

"You let him out. . . . Anything else?"

Joe raised his hand again. "What if Beau won't leave? He says he likes eatin' regular like when he's in jail."

"Take five bucks out of petty cash and buy him a pint. He'd rather drink than eat any day. Just tell him he can't drink it in town. But don't let him have his truck. Make him walk."

Lansing wiped his mouth. "If that's it, I'm on my way."

The sheriff paid for his breakfast at the counter and headed out the door. He paused before crossing the street to let a Jeep pass. The passenger in the Jeep looked familiar, but he couldn't place a name with the face. He shrugged it off and started across the square for the courthouse.

# 16

THE DRIVE SOUTH OF LAS PALMAS WAS PLEASANT. LONGTREE talked about growing up on the Navajo reservation. Both of his parents had been educated at the university. They could have moved to the big city and had what most Americans would consider normal, middle-class lives. They opted for returning to the reservation and helping their people. They were schoolteachers.

"I learned at an early age the value of an education," the lawyer elaborated. "I also learned, no matter how much education you had, it didn't help one bit if there were no jobs to be had . . . and I didn't want a career weaving blankets.

"My folks instilled in me the need to help my people. What they didn't realize is that you can't just work the system from the inside. That's why I moved off the reservation and became a lawyer. All the rules and regulations that limit Native American prosperity are dictated from beyond the borders of our lands by whites who have never seen a reservation."

"You speak of your parents in the past tense," Williston observed.

"My father died of a stroke about five years ago. High blood pressure. My mother died this past year.

The virus outbreak. The one the Centers for Disease Control said was spread by fleas and rats."

"I'm sorry," Williston apologized.

"One of the great tragedies of living on a reservation, Senator. That's why I'm interested in the land swap. Even though I was raised Navajo, half my relatives are Zuni on my mother's side. Education is only half the battle against poverty. The other half is opportunity. Developing an additional two hundred thousand acres may help kick-start the Zuni economy. Who knows? It won't hurt."

Williston tried to think of a gentlemanly way of asking Longtree what kind of deal McGaffrey had offered. Whatever the proposal, the senator suspected the lawyer was not driven by greed or personal gain.

Longtree slowed his Jeep and turned off the highway. The one-lane dirt road they were now on dipped into a wide, flat valley. Williston could see the road ahead as it wound its way up the slope of the valley's far side, then disappeared out of view.

At first they were traveling east, straight into the sun. Once through the valley, the road turned them to the north. They were pointed at the rugged hill country that marked the southern boundary of the Anasazi Strip.

Longtree did his best to avoid the larger rocks. Occasionally the front bumper of the Jeep sheared off the tops of pear cactus trying to reclaim the arid land. The senator could tell by the size of the cactus plants that the road was seldom used.

Williston turned to look back toward the highway. Route 15 had already disappeared behind the hills. Even the power lines that paralleled the highway could not be seen. He turned to the driver. "How much farther?"

"Another twenty, thirty minutes." He pointed ahead

and toward the right. "You see that second hill with boulders on top, no trees?"

"Yeah."

"We'll stop just this side of it."

"How far is that?"

"'Bout ten miles."

Williston never ceased to be amazed at how hard it was to judge distances in that grand, open country called New Mexico. There was a time in his youth when his guesses were fairly close. It was a skill he had let lapse. It was a skill he wished he had time to reacquire.

Williston tried to keep the hill marking their destination in sight, but the winding road made that impossible. After one series of turns the hill would appear in front of them. They would round a boulder after two or three more turns and the hill would be to their left. The next time it was to their right. Williston gave up. He settled back in his seat and enjoyed the ride. The landscape was rapidly changing from rolling desert to hills and boulders decorated with piñon trees and leafy, flowering plants. As they climbed higher into the hills, the heat from the valleys below subsided slightly.

The Jeep rounded another turn. "Here we are," Longtree announced.

The road came to an abrupt end in a broad, flat area at the base of the hill Williston had been watching. A small adobe shack, shaded by a lone juniper, sat at the far end of the tiny valley. Longtree parked the Jeep under the tree. The two men got out. Williston was grateful for the chance to stretch.

"Wait here," Longtree ordered. The lawyer went into the shack.

Williston glanced at his watch. It was nine o'clock. The trip had taken almost two hours. The senator shrugged off Longtree's miscalculation. He had enjoyed the drive.

Longtree emerged from the hut. "He's not here."

"What now?" the senator asked, removing his hat to wipe the band.

"We wait." Longtree grabbed the water thermos from the backseat. "Might as well go inside. It's a lot cooler in there."

Williston followed him into the shack.

The adobe hut was a single room. The exterior door was built of rough-hewn wood held together by wooden pegs. It swung easily on leather hinges. The walls were almost two feet thick. The result was no direct sunlight penetrated the doorway or single, paneless window to interfere with the cool, inviting interior.

The plaster-and-rock roof was supported by timbers running the length of the room. The bark had been removed from the beams, but no other workmanship had been applied to the wood. In one corner was a hearth. Stone seats along the walls had been incorporated into the construction. A single mat, woven from agave fibers, adorned the floor. The mat was large enough to serve as a sleeping pallet. There were no other furnishings.

After studying the room for a moment, the feature that struck Williston the most was that the building could have been standing for over five hundred years. There was no influence from the white man. No forged metal: no nails, no hinges, no hint of implements. There was no glass in the single window.

"The Watcher lives a very Spartan existence," Williston commented.

"I don't think he has been here in a very long time," Longtree guessed, taking a seat against the wall.

"When was the last time you saw him?" Williston asked, kneeling to feel the texture of the woven mat.

"One . . . two years."

Williston looked up. "If you haven't seen him in two years, how did you know he wanted to meet with me?"

"The elders of the tribe told me."

"When was that?"

"Last week, when they heard you were coming to Santa Fe."

"Did you tell them I agreed to meet with Windwalker?"

"No. I didn't have time."

Williston stood. "You dragged me up here for nothing!" he snapped angrily. "This Watcher of yours has no idea about this meeting or that I'm even here!"

"That is not true," came a calm voice from behind the senator. Williston turned to the door. There was the figure of a man, silhouetted by the bright morning sun, in the opening. "I have known for some time you would come."

Longtree stood. "Senator Carter Williston . . . I would like you to meet Joseph Windwalker."

Williston stood gaping, trying to overcome surprise, embarrassment, and disbelief. Windwalker broke the silence. "I am pleased to finally meet you, Senator Williston." The old man stepped into the room.

"I—I am pleased to meet you, Mr. Windwalker." Williston extended his hand. Windwalker acknowledged the proffered hand by bowing slightly, but he did not shake hands.

Williston studied the man standing in front of him. He was much shorter than Williston. Maybe five foot four, the senator guessed. Windwalker was old. Too old for adequate description, Williston thought. The lines on the Watcher's face were deep and weather-beaten. The old man's hair was long and white. The eyes were black and flashed like polished obsidian. He was dressed simply in linen trousers, a baggy linen shirt, and moccasins. Apparently Windwalker's only concession to the white man's influence was the dark brown, wide-brimmed hat that he wore.

Windwalker was direct. "We have a great deal to discuss, Senator."

"I agree." Williston nodded, dropping his hand awkwardly. "Would you care to sit down?" He indicated one of the stone seats.

"It is inappropriate that we speak here. Do you ride?"

"Ride?" Williston was confused.

"Horses."

"Yes. Yes, I do."

"We will go then." He turned to Longtree. "Will you wait for Senator Williston?"

"You don't need me to come along?" the lawyer asked, disappointment in his voice.

"No," the elder man responded with an air of finality.

"Then, yes," Longtree concluded, "I will wait for Senator Williston."

The Watcher turned to Williston. "Come."

Williston followed Windwalker from the hut. Two ponies waited for them behind the shack. Neither had a saddle and there were no bridles. Each had only a rope tied loosely around the neck.

Windwalker approached the nearest horse. Taking the rope in one hand, he easily swung himself onto the back of the pony. Williston tried to follow his example. There was a momentary struggle. The senator floundered with one leg on the pony's back before he slipped to the ground. He tried again, this time flopping his stomach across the horse's back, then swinging his right leg over the rear. A second later he was sitting upright on his mount.

Windwalker grunted, satisfied his guest was ready

to follow. The Watcher pointed his horse toward the arroyo that descended from the hills behind the shack. With no coaxing from Williston, the second pony followed.

# 17

LANSING PARKED HIS TRUCK AND HORSE TRAILER NEAR THE spot where Beau Watson's truck had been found. The crime scene had been picked clean of all the evidence Stu Ortega thought pertinent. The sheriff walked casually around the area to see if something obvious had been overlooked. There was still a small piece of pottery tucked under a sage bush. Lansing picked it up, and after studying it a moment, dropped it into his shirt pocket.

After scanning from that area to the spot where he found Duke Semple's body, Lansing was satisfied nothing else had been left behind. He walked to the back of the horse trailer and let down the gate.

"Come on, Cement Head," he said, backing his horse down the ramp. "The free ride's over."

He wrapped the reins loosely around the truck's bumper. Reaching inside his cab, he grabbed his rifle, canteen, and saddlebag. He slipped the rifle into the saddle holster, hooked the canteen over the horn, and flopped the saddlebag over Cement Head's back. Using small leather straps on the back of the saddle, he tied the bag securely. Before leaving, he made sure the truck was locked.

Unwrapping the reins, the sheriff swung himself

into the saddle. "All right, Cement Head, let's go for a little ride." Lansing pointed his horse toward the foothills to the east.

During the numerous conversations Lansing had had with Beau, the ranch hand kept talking about the site he and Duke had been excavating. The closest they could get their truck to the Indian ruins was about three quarters of a mile. He talked about having to hoof it over a hill. The ruins were on the other side.

Lansing directed the horse toward the nearest hill. He kept the pace slow so he could study the ground. The earth was hard-packed and stony. It was impossible to pick out footprints. The hill was low with a gradual slope. Walking up or down the slight grade would take little effort. Lansing continued his slow scan of the rocky earth until he reached the top of the hill.

Below him on the bottom of a broad, flat basin was the distinct outline of an ancient Indian village. Time and the elements had left little of the original buildings. Only the geometric patterns showing the foundations of long-forgotten homes and ritual kivas remained.

Lansing nudged the horse with his heels and they trotted gently down the hill.

The high desert had sought to reclaim the village, trying to erase any evidence of humanity. After a thousand years of wind, rain, and sand fashioning the village to match the surrounding terrain, it was easy for Lansing to find the spot most recently disturbed by man.

The two range hands had concentrated their digging on one of the kivas, the round, nearly subterranean ceremonial chambers that served as centerpieces of Anasazi religion and culture. That made sense to Lansing. The other buildings would have been built aboveground. Pottery and other artifacts would have been destroyed by the elements, just as the buildings had. The contents of the kiva would have been buried by the desert sands, preserving them in reasonably good condition. It was obvious to the sheriff that Beau and Duke had a great deal of experience raping ancient sites.

Lansing dismounted short of the ruins and tied the reins around the branch of a scrub sage. Finding footprints in the ruins was easy. Because the earth had been disturbed by man a millennium before, the soil was looser, comprised of blown sand and dirt. It was still hard-packed but it wasn't mingled with rocks and pebbles.

The ring of the kiva was forty feet in diameter. Lansing found boot tracks throughout the interior. Four pits had been dug near the walls of the structure. The sheriff wasn't sure how deep the pits had been. The intruders had made a vain attempt at filling them. Mixed in the fill dirt were several small pottery shards, samples that did not meet specifications.

The earth within the kiva ruins was too disturbed to determine how many people had tracked through it. Lansing started studying the ground surrounding the ceremonial pit. He found three sets of boot tracks on the western side leading from the hill. That checked with Beau's story. Duke had walked back to the kiva to retrieve the pick and shovel. Only two sets of boot tracks led back to the hill.

Duke made it to the kiva a second time, Lansing surmised, but he didn't walk back. At least, not the way he had come. Lansing began a slow walk around the ruin's perimeter.

On the south side of the kiva were the tracks the sheriff had hoped to find. Boot marks were dug into the sand, as if the owner had been running. Twenty feet beyond the rim of the kiva, two other sets of boot marks converged on the first. Someone was chasing him, Lansing thought. The chase had continued into the sagebrush. The ground was getting harder with fewer tracks to follow.

The sheriff stopped and looked to either side of the fading trail. Several pieces of clear glass glistened from beneath a sage plant. Lansing knelt to examine them. The larger pieces were thin and curved. The glass wasn't thick enough to come from a bottle or jar, Lansing thought. It could have been from the glass casing of the Coleman lantern Beau and Duke had. There was no sign of the lantern.

Lansing returned to the boot tracks. They continued a little farther, then stopped at a spot that could have been the scene of a struggle. The footprints faced in all directions and the surface of the ground was torn up. The tracks didn't go any farther into the desert.

Lansing walked back to the kiva, satisfied there was no more evidence on that side of the ruins.

"What do you think, Cement Head?" Lansing asked. "We have enough proof to show someone else was here. Should we go back to town and spring Beau or keep on looking for the bad guys?"

Cement Head looked up from the sagebrush he was nibbling on, snorted and turned his attention back to the plant.

"That's just like you. Always wanting to go after the bad guys." Lansing untied his horse and led him around the far side of the kiva. On the eastern side of the village the sheriff found more boot tracks. There were still more signs of a struggle. There was also a darkened blotch of sand. Lansing suspected it was dried blood. He removed a zippered plastic bag from a saddlebag and scraped some of the sand into it. Sealing the bag, he returned it to the leather pouch.

The new sets of boot tracks led to the east. Lansing followed them, leading his horse, until he came to a patch of ground torn up by horse hooves. Lansing turned to his companion. "Looks like I get to ride for a while." He swung himself into the saddle and started following the trail.

The new trail took him farther into the hills. It was easy to follow. Two miles from the Indian ruins, Lansing found himself on top of a rise overlooking a wide gulch, carved into the desert by runoff from the hills. The gulch was dry. Its bottom was wide and smooth from the sediment left by the occasional river that passed through it.

A half mile from where Lansing sat was a clump of cottonwood trees. The trail he was following led to the bottom of the gulch and down the streambed. At the bottom of the gulch he could see beneath the trees. Parked in the shade, and hidden from casual view, was a truck and a double-wide horse trailer.

"Cement Head," Lansing whispered, "you don't suppose that truck belongs to the bad guys, do you?"

The horse shook his head, trying to shoo flies away.

"You're not right all the time," Lansing observed. He unsnapped the strap holding his pistol secure in its holster. "Come on." He spurred the horse gently with his heels and approached the truck.

As he grew nearer, he realized there was no one around. He double-checked to make sure the trail he was following led to the trees. It did, but another set of tracks was headed farther into the hill country.

Lansing studied the creek bed. There were double sets of tire tracks in the sand. This truck, or another one like it pulling a trailer, had been there before. He got off his horse to inspect the truck. It was locked. There was nothing inside the trailer to arouse suspicion.

He pulled a pen and a small writing pad from the saddlebag and jotted down the license plate numbers of the truck and trailer. "Let's go, old buddy," Lansing said to his horse. "Looks like we're not finished yet."

He pointed his horse toward the hill country and took up the new trail.

# 18

WINDWALKER WAS LEADING WILLISTON FARTHER AND FARther into the hill country. The senator kept wondering why they were called hills. They might be hills compared to the peaks along the Continental Divide, but they were mountains to the senator.

The arroyo behind the cabin had grown steep very quickly. Before long they were crossing a ridge and descending into a canyon. Williston could not tell how far they traveled along the canyon floor before the trail led them up to its rim.

Windwalker said nothing, ignoring all of the senator's queries. This, at least, gave Williston time to consider his situation. This was not what he had expected. He assumed the Watcher, Longtree, and he would sit down, smoke a peace pipe, maybe, then he would explain all the advantages of the land swap. He had even considered throwing a new Cadillac into the deal for Windwalker. Surely the old Zuni would jump at such an offer.

Williston looked over the edge of the canyon they were paralleling. It was two hundred feet to the bottom of the gorge. He wondered if Daniel Patrick Moynihan ever ended up in a situation like this.

The senator looked at his watch. It read eleven

o'clock. "Windwalker, if you don't mind my asking . . . We've been at this for over two hours. How much farther?"

"Not far," was the only response the Watcher would give.

Their course soon had them descending into yet another ravine. The route was nothing more than an animal trail worn into the side of the steep canyon walls. Despite Williston's doubts, he had to admit the pony he was riding seemed surefooted enough for the narrow path they were following. It took ten minutes to reach the bottom. The floor of the gorge was sandy and flat, around twenty feet across. Small pools of water, left from the last rain, huddled beneath overhanging rocks. This only served to remind Williston he'd had nothing to drink for hours.

About the time Williston was again going to ask how much farther, Windwalker stopped his horse. Slipping to the ground, he signaled Williston to do the same. It took the senator's legs a moment to get their steadiness once he was standing. While Williston readjusted to gravity, Windwalker led the ponies to a clump of small willow trees. He tied their ropes so the animals could reach a nearby pool of standing water.

Windwalker turned to the senator. "I have brought you to this place so you can understand what I tell you. The legends of my people make pleasant stories for the white man. But that is all they are: stories. And so I have brought you here so you can see what I tell you is true."

Windwalker turned and started walking up a small wash that fed into the canyon. Williston followed. As they climbed higher, Williston saw the origin of the occasional stream. Fifty feet above the creek bed was a fracture in the canyon wall. The senator didn't discover the opening until they were almost next to it.

The entrance was no more than a thin crack in the

native rock, closed at the top. Windwalker had to turn sideways to slip through. Asking no questions, Williston followed the old man.

The cave was high enough for a man to remain upright. Williston kept his eye on his guide. Windwalker remained in sight for the first twenty feet, then disappeared around a sharp turn in the rock. Williston hurried to catch him. The dim light from the entrance did not illuminate the next part of the passage. Williston stopped for a moment to let his eyes adjust. Fifty feet ahead was the dim glow of reflected light against the rock walls. The senator saw the shadowy movement of Windwalker at the far end of the rocky corridor.

Williston continued down the passage, only mildly enjoying the pleasantly cool rock walls. When he reached the second turn in the passage, he realized he was in a tunnel, not a cave. Another fifty feet ahead was a third turn, illuminated by an outside opening.

Windwalker was waiting for the senator outside the passageway. Williston had to shield his eyes against the noon sun and it was a moment before he could discern the new surroundings. He soon realized they had passed from one canyon to another. They stood on the floor of the new canyon, comprised of sheer sandstone cliffs.

Williston gaped at the spectacle in front of them. Along the opposite wall from where they stood was the most massive Anasazi cliff dwelling Williston had ever seen. It had been years since he'd been to the Cliff Palace at Mesa Verde National Park, but this new discovery had to be twice that size.

"I can't believe it," Williston whispered. "This is the most impressive thing I've ever seen. What is this place?"

"Come," Windwalker ordered, ignoring the question. The old man started for the base of the cliff below the sandstone city. Williston obeyed.

The canyon was no more than a hundred yards across and they quickly reached the base of the cliff. Sets of handholds and toeholds were carved into the rock. Windwalker started climbing immediately. The white man waited until his guide had climbed ten feet before he followed.

Williston could only guess how far above the canyon floor they climbed before reaching the cliff dwelling's ledge. It was at least seventy-five feet. When he finally stood on the sandstone ledge that served as the foundation for all the structures, Williston began to grasp the size of the small city. The rocky overhang that protected the dwellings was another hundred feet above his head. The back wall of the massive recess was almost two hundred feet from the canyon wall.

The stone and mortar buildings were eight stories high. It was a moment of overwhelming discovery when Williston realized he was not looking at ruins. The buildings looked new. "What is this place?"

"In the ancient tongue, it was called *Itiwana,* the Center of the Universe."

"Can we look inside?"

"Not yet, Senator Williston. We must talk with the *a'doshle,*" Windwalker explained. "They must know why you are here."

"Who are the *a'doshle*?"

"They will reveal themselves to you. . . . Come." The round outlines of several kiva roofs formed the plaza in front of the living quarters. The diameters of the kivas varied from thirty to forty feet. In the center of each kiva roof was a single opening, the only access into each chamber. Windwalker proceeded to the largest kiva. Almost fifty feet across, it was located at the center of the other kivas. The Watcher descended into the ceremonial chamber by way of a wooden ladder.

Williston looked into the opening. Once he was sure Windwalker was clear, the senator climbed into the pit. The ceiling at the apex was eighteen feet in height. The roof tapered down to the supporting walls five feet high. The interior was dark, the only light coming from the opening in the roof.

Looking around the room, Williston found his host seated on a stone seat along the wall. It reminded him of the stone seats at the adobe shack. The Watcher indicated Williston should sit next to him.

As his eyes grew accustomed to the dim light, Williston surveyed the interior of the chamber. Along the walls, painted on the plaster coating, were pictographs and undecipherable symbols describing a long-dead culture. The colors, even in the dull light, were still brilliant: reds, blacks, yellow ochers. Utensils of everyday life sat on mats woven from yucca fibers. There were bowls, stone knives, shell- and turquoise-adorned jewelry. Along the walls leaned the implements of war: bows and arrows, battle clubs, spears, the spear launchers known as atlatls. To Williston the arrangement of the items looked like a display in a museum.

Williston could think of nothing to say or ask. He was overwhelmed by a deep reverence for the sacred chamber. He sat and waited for Windwalker to break the silence.

The Watcher closed his eyes. With his palms facing upward, the old man began a quiet chant. The words were foreign to Williston. He sat quietly, waiting for the shaman to end his ceremony.

From beneath his stone seat the senator felt a rumble, like distant thunder. He looked to the Indian to see if he felt it. The Watcher continued his chant. The thunder became more distinct, more audible. The chamber started becoming darker as if clouds were blocking the sunlight.

Mixed with the sound of the increasing thunder came the sound of the wind. It began slowly, then gained more intensity as the chamber became even darker. The wind began whipping through the opening of the kiva. Dust and sand, stirred by the violent breeze, kicked up from the floor.

Williston had to shield his eyes from the whirlwind that enveloped the entire room. In the dust and darkness, above the sound of the wailing wind, came new voices, chanting in unison with the Watcher. Williston squinted his eyes open to find who had joined them. In the center of the chamber were three figures, as tall as the kiva roof, wearing ceremonial robes elaborately decorated in feathers and fur, wheeling around in a strange, contorted dance. The faces were grotesque and distorted. At one point the most gruesome of the three stopped his gyrations and turned to Williston, fixing him with a chilling stare.

An uncontrollable shiver ran through the white man. He wanted to run but his limbs were so heavy he couldn't move. The unrelenting wind peppered his eyes and he had to squeeze them shut. After a moment, he forced himself to look at the demons one more time. The figures were still there, behind them dozens of other figures, their hideous faces gauzed by the flying sand.

He pressed his palms against his eyes to block the nightmare. He couldn't open his mouth because of the whirling dust, but in his mind he was screaming: "Stop. *Stop. Stop!*"

Suddenly, it came to an end. The silence was deafening.

Williston pulled his palms from his eyes and looked around the room. The sunlight poured through the kiva's door. The wind was gone. The demons had left.

"The *a'doshle* have looked into your heart, Senator Williston," Windwalker said quietly. "They have seen your virtue. You are welcome here."

# 19

"WHO ARE THE *A'DOSHLE*?" WILLISTON ASKED QUIETLY, STILL trying to recover from the vision he had experienced.

"They are the spirits who protect this place. Did they reveal themselves to you?"

"Maybe more than I wished . . ." His voice trailed off.

"That is good." The Watcher nodded. "That is very good. Now we can talk. Now we can talk and you will believe." The kiva was quiet, except for the sound of Joseph Windwalker's voice.

"When the Great Spirit created the earth, all was darkness and all the creatures lived together in the darkness inside the earth. It was the beginning of creation. The world outside the earth was cold and dark, as well. But the Spirit saw his creatures were not happy in the darkness, so he created the Sun Spirit. The Sun Spirit melted the ice above the earth and gave light.

"Then the Great Spirit made a hole in the earth and a ladder and bade his creatures come from the earth to see what he had made. All of the Spirit's creatures rejoiced, but only Human Beings thanked him. And because Human Beings thanked him, the Spirit gave them the gift of the *Shipap,* so they would not forget.

"The kiva was our sacred place, to remind ourselves from where we came. Wherever we built our dwellings, there was always the kiva, to remind ourselves of the *Shipap*.

"For ten thousand summers, since the beginning of time, the Human Beings kept faith with the Great Spirit. To honor our ancestors, each son was taught to remember the names of his family and to recite them on the day he entered manhood. Because all creatures were our brothers, born of the *Shipap*, we always gave thanks to their spirits that their lives gave us sustenance.

"The Humans were strong and good. They built many cities and prospered because they kept faith. They befriended many people and taught them the ways of the Great Spirit.

"Then the Children of the Serpent came to live among the Humans. The Children of the Serpent learned the ways of the Great Spirit. But they did not believe in the *Shipap*. They said the one true Spirit was the Sun. They said the Spirit of the Sun could live only if he was given the blood of Human Beings. They said the Sun would die and all would be darkness. The Children of the Serpent told the Humans if they sacrificed their brothers, they would be as gods, holding power over life and death.

"The Humans believed the Children of the Serpent and did not want to live in darkness. So they killed their brothers and sisters, and sacrificed their blood to the Sun Spirit.

"This made the Great Spirit angry, because his children forgot the way of the *Shipap* and the peace they had known. Because the Human Beings had thought they, too, could be as the gods, the *a'doshle* came in a whirlwind. They dried the crops, drove the men from their sacred kivas, and erased from the Human Beings the memory of the *Shipap*."

Windwalker sat silent for a moment.

"What became of the Human Beings?" Williston ventured to ask.

"They were sent to live with the scorpion in the desert. The ground was made barren so the crops would not grow. Their great kivas were buried in the blowing sands and their houses fell down."

"What about the Children of the Serpent?"

"They were driven far to the south. There they built great cities and monuments to their Sun Spirit. They conquered many people so they could make sacrifices to the Sun Spirit."

"You're talking about the Aztecs."

Windwalker nodded. "The Children of the Serpent made the Great Spirit angry. So he created the White Man and sent him across the waters to destroy the Aztec. The Children of the Serpent were made slaves to the White Man and could not sacrifice their brothers ever again."

Williston wanted to smile over the naive explanation of how the White Man came to the New World, but he thought better of it. The memory of the *a'doshle* staring into his soul was too fresh. Instead, he asked, "When were the Human Beings driven from here?"

"The life cycle of a Human is fifty-two summers. This is the fourteenth year of the fourteenth cycle."

Williston tried to do a quick calculation: 52 years times 13 life cycles was 676 years, plus 14 was 690. *They were driven out around 1300, give or take a few years,* he thought to himself. *What was it McGaffrey said? The Aztec didn't show up in Mexico until 1325.*

Despite his inclination to discount Windwalker's fable, the historical timing was too precise to ignore completely.

Windwalker continued. "The *a'doshle* foretold the *Shipap* would be secure for thirteen cycles. Then, in the fourteenth year of the fourteenth cycle a man will come who owns many souls. This man will challenge the *a'doshle* and destroy the *Shipap.*"

"I haven't come to destroy the *Shipap.*"

"It is not you, Senator Carter Williston. You are not the Destroyer. You are not the buyer and seller of men's souls."

"Why can't your *a'doshle* stop him?"

"The *a'doshle* are spirits who draw their strength through the faith of the believers. But the believers are few now, and the *a'doshle* have grown weak. Only the man who has lost his soul can stop the Destroyer, because he has nothing else to fear." Windwalker stood. "Come. You are thirsty."

In the wonder and excitement of the past hour, Williston had forgotten his need for something to drink. The craving was suddenly overpowering. He followed Windwalker up the ladder.

The old Indian walked across the plaza to the nearest of the apartment dwellings. Williston had to stoop to get through the door. The room was small, ten feet on a side, with only a six-foot ceiling. There was a small window facing outside, as well as the entry door. A second door on the back wall led to an interior apartment. The room they were in appeared to be a kitchen. A mano, a millstone shaped like a rolling pin, sat on the curved surface of a stone metate, abandoned seven hundred years before by a long-forgotten Anasazi housewife. The maize she had been grinding had long since turned to dust. Various bowls and vessels for liquids, herbs, and spices were neatly placed in niches in the walls, ready for use.

Windwalker went to the back corner of the room and removed a round stone from a hole in the floor. He handed the senator a ladle made from a hollowed gourd, then gestured toward the hole.

Williston knelt and looked into the recess. Water, captured in a cistern, reflected his image ten inches below the opening. From deep within the ancient houses came the faint sound of dripping water, filtering through an elaborate delivery system.

He dipped the gourd into the water and sniffed it. The water was clear and there were no strange odors. He ventured a sip. The water was cool and refreshing. He quickly finished the contents of the gourd and refilled it for a second and third drink.

The senator sat on the floor with his back against the wall. "Where does the water come from?"

"The rains. It seeps through the rocks of the mountains," Windwalker explained. "The Human Beings baked clay tiles and laid them in the holding wells so the water would not escape."

"Ingenious," Williston said in wonder. "Can I see more of this place?"

Windwalker nodded. The two men stepped through the door leading to the interior apartment. The room was almost dark, the only light coming from the door to the kitchen and a hole in the ceiling. A ladder provided access through the ceiling to yet another apartment. Williston followed his guide to the next level.

The upstairs apartment was better lit, with a large exterior window overlooking the plaza. Williston guessed the new room was used as a sleeping quarters. Three thick mats, similar to the pallet he had seen in the adobe shack, were arranged on the floor. There were brightly colored blankets folded on the mats. Williston reached to touch one, then looked at Windwalker to see if it was permitted. The *Kiaklo* nodded.

The senator picked up the blanket. The color was primarily red, with rich blue, yellow, and green patterns woven into the fabric. The patterns were not unlike the types Williston had seen on modern samples. The fabric itself was a heavy cotton of some kind. "This is beautiful," Williston commented. He wanted to say it would be worth thousands of dollars, but he didn't think his host would appreciate the observation.

He returned the blanket to the mat. The pottery and other vessels Williston found in the room were decorated with ornate black-and-white figures. The baskets were meticulously woven from sturdy yucca fiber. Everything was as it had been left seven centuries earlier. Each item was perfectly preserved.

The two men followed the maze of ladders and interlocking apartments. Each room told the same story. Windwalker explained how each family had their own set of rooms for eating and sleeping. It was the kiva that was the heart of the culture. Each clan maintained its own kiva for social and religious activity.

"You said the kiva was built to remind the Anasazi of the *Shipap*. Have you ever seen the *Shipap*?" Williston asked as they climbed from the highest level of apartments.

"No living Human Being has seen the *Shipap*." Windwalker shook his head. "The memory of the sacred place was taken from the Humans when they were driven from the kiva."

"Do you think it truly existed?"

"The *a'doshle* still haunt this land, protecting it from those who would disturb it. Why would they do that if it didn't exist?"

Williston didn't have a quick answer for that one. Instead, he asked, "What do you want of me?"

"The Great Spirit created the White Man to punish the Human Beings. The White Man has taken our land, taught us their ways, and forced us to forget our ancient traditions. The Children of the *Shipap* are clinging to life. If the *Shipap* falls into the hands of the Destroyer, the Children will die. Even though you are a White Man, I ask you: Do not let that happen!"

"You talk in circles, Windwalker, but all right," Williston agreed. "I will do my best not to let the Destroyer have the *Shipap*."

With Windwalker leading the way, the two emerged onto the plaza, dotted with the entrances of the many kivas.

"It's about time!" growled a rough voice. "We've been waiting for you."

# 20

TWO MEN STOOD FIFTY FEET FROM WHERE WILLISTON AND Windwalker had exited the lower-tier apartment. The strangers were equipped with side arms and rifles. One rifle was an M-16, the other a longer range Winchester. Both rifles were leveled at the senator and the Zuni.

"Move away from that door," the man with the Winchester ordered. "And keep your hands where I can see them." He motioned them away from the dwellings using the muzzle of his rifle as a pointer.

"What do you want?" Williston demanded, standing his ground.

"We don't want anything from you, mister," the self-appointed spokesman said. "We came to talk to your Indian friend there."

Williston looked at Windwalker, then back at the gunmen. "What do you want to talk to him about?"

"It's a personal matter that doesn't concern you. So why don't you just shut up!"

"Friend, I don't think you know who you're dealing with." Williston tried to indicate with his tone of voice he wasn't taking crap from anyone.

"I said shut up, *'friend',*" the speaker growled. "I think you forget I'm the one with a gun."

Before Williston could respond, Windwalker dove

into him, knocking him through the entrance to the apartment, onto the floor.

"Stop!" It was the voice of the second gunman. The blast from his M-16 echoed through the canyon. The bullets ripped through the doorway, shattering sandstone chips from the interior walls.

"Climb," Windwalker ordered, getting up from on top of Williston. "Hurry. And pull the ladder up behind you."

"What?" the dazed senator asked.

"Climb!" Windwalker repeated. The *Kiaklo* disappeared through a doorway leading to an apartment further back.

Williston heard the scuffing of boots on sandstone as the gunmen ran toward the dwelling. Without checking to see how close they were, the senator scrambled up the ladder to the room above. He pulled the ladder through the opening as the men entered below.

"Up there!" one of them shouted. The man with the M-16 sent a burst through the opening.

Williston ducked into the adjoining apartment. There was no access to the upper level from that room, but there was another doorway. He didn't wait to see if he was being followed. He hurried into the next chamber. Another ladder led to the next higher tier. Climbing as quickly as he could, Williston pulled his feet clear of the opening, then pulled the ladder up.

Williston stopped for a moment to catch his breath. With the apartment ceilings only six feet high, removing the ladders would be only a minor inconvenience for the gunmen. They could easily hoist themselves through. For that matter, once they had pulled themselves up to the second level, they could bring that ladder with them. That gave Williston an idea.

He passed through two more apartments before he found another portal to the next higher tier. Instead of climbing the ladder, he pushed it upward, onto the next level. He then dove through a door that led to an interior apartment.

The light was dim, but he could see the dark outline of yet another opening. He hurried through it.

Williston found himself engulfed in darkness. The chamber was cool, but musty. As he felt his way along the walls, searching for an exit, the sandstone seemed damp to the touch.

The senator listened for any pursuit. Behind him, everything was quiet. As he continued his groping exploration he remembered an axiom about mazes. Pick a wall, either left or right, and follow that one wall. Eventually you will come to the exit. For no reason, Williston chose the wall to his left.

He passed from one chamber into the next. He moved slowly so that he wouldn't fall through a doorway. His concentration was so fixed on following the walls, he forgot about the openings in the floors. He let out an involuntary yell as he fell to the room below.

Williston clamped his hand over his mouth, as if the action would rescind the cry he had just made. He listened in the darkness for any response. When none came, he checked himself for damage. Somehow or other he hadn't hurt himself.

Groping for the wall, he began his systematic search for an exit. Feeling his way from one chamber to the next and staying clear of holes in the floor, he eventually saw the dim glow of daylight ahead. He hurried to the light.

The room he entered had a small window that looked out over the plaza. Williston crept on all fours to the opening. Easing his view over the sill, he could see no movement. He raised himself a little farther. Somehow he had worked his way to the southern end of the dwellings. He was positioned just above the stone ladder that led from the valley floor to the sandstone shelf. He was less than fifty feet from freedom.

From his vantage point, Williston could see the entire length of the plaza. Movement in the doorway in one of the far apartments caught his attention. It was Windwalker. The old man peeked from his hiding place. Checking both directions first, the ancient Zuni stepped from the doorway and began a slow trot toward the edge of the cliff.

The shattering sound of automatic gunfire reverberated through the ancient dwellings. Bullets tore at the rock floor around Windwalker's feet.

Williston shifted his view to a second-tier window. The man with the M-16 was spewing bullets at the old man.

"Stop!" Williston shouted, forcing himself through the window, onto the roof of the next lower apartment. "Stop it!"

The gunfire stopped. Williston looked toward the edge of the rock shelf. Windwalker was gone.

"You can hold it right there."

Williston raised his hands and turned. The man with the Winchester stood on a landing twenty feet away and one tier higher.

"Reid!" the man bellowed.

"Yeah, Hatch. I'm right here." Reid had appeared through the doorway of a bottom apartment.

"Where's the old man?"

"I think he jumped." The man named Reid edged closer to the rim of the cliff. "I don't see nothin', 'cept his hat blowin' around down there."

Williston realized then that he had lost his own hat.

"Guess we'll go down and take a look." Hatch motioned with his rifle for Williston to climb down from the apartment roof. "This way, Senator."

Williston was surprised. "You know who I am?"

"Oh, yeah. I know who you are," Hatch admitted. "I just don't know what to do with you."

Williston sat uncomfortably with his back against the canyon wall. Hatch rested against a boulder twenty feet away smoking a cigarette, his gun still pointed at the senator. Williston tried several times to ask his captor what the whole thing was about. Hatch either ignored the questions or told him to be quiet. Eventually, Reid came trudging up the canyon floor carrying Windwalker's hat.

"Well?" Hatch asked.

"I didn't find nothin'." Reid sounded exasperated. "Maybe when we shot 'im he fell on a ledge or somethin'. But I can't see nothin' from down here. . . . Or maybe he crawled off under a bush somewhere. Want me to go back and look?"

"No." Hatch shook his head. "Even if he survived the fall he'll be too busted up to last long. Let's just go. I don't want to get lost in these canyons after dark." He motioned with his rifle for Williston to get up. "Come on, Senator."

Williston stood. "Where're we going?"

"You'll find out soon enough. Start heading for that tunnel over there." Hatch indicated the entry to the canyon Williston and Windwalker had used earlier.

When they reached the entrance, Hatch told Reid to keep the gun on Williston while he went through the tunnel. The two waited for a minute. "Send him through, Reid," came the muted order from the far end of the passage.

"Okay, Senator. Get goin'," Reid commanded.

Williston went into the tunnel. Reid waited until ten feet separated them before following.

The senator thought quickly. When he made the turn into the fifty-foot dark section of passage, no one would have a gun on him. There was a chance Reid would not be expecting him to make a grab for the M-16. Williston quickened his pace to put more separation between the two.

Reid either didn't notice or didn't care, just as long as the senator was well in front.

Williston turned the corner into the long corridor. The passage was still narrow, but not too narrow for him to turn and crouch. The dark figure of Reid came around the corner. Williston leaped for the gun.

Reid's finger was on the trigger and the weapon was set on automatic fire.

Williston pushed the muzzle of the rifle toward the roof as the tunnel was sprayed with a hail of bullets. The reverberation of the discharging weapon and ricocheting projectiles was deafening.

Reid was thrown against the far wall of the tunnel from Williston's charge. Williston tried to wrest the gun from him, but the younger man's grip was too secure. It took the gunman only a second to recover. A moment later he had Williston forced against the opposite wall of the passage. The rifle Williston had tried to grab was now shoved against his throat and the senator found himself gasping for breath.

Reid let one hand release the rifle. His right hand free, he gave Williston a terrific blow to the solar plexus.

Everything went black for Williston for a moment. He found himself sitting on the passageway floor struggling to breathe. Somewhere behind him Hatch asked, "What the hell's going on in here?"

"Son of a bitch tried to jump me," Reid chuckled.

"You shoot him?"

"Naw, not this time." He continued to chuckle. "But I did show 'im he's not as tough as he thinks he is." He gave Williston a hard kick in the ribs. "Come on, Mr. Politician. Get up."

Holding his ribs, Williston managed to stand. He

stumbled down the corridor with Reid pushing him from behind.

Williston was still trying to catch his breath when they emerged from the tunnel. Hatch was already halfway to the bottom of the canyon when they started down. "You can move faster than that!" Reid snorted. He gave Williston a shove. Williston tripped and began rolling down the hill. He skidded nearly to Hatch's feet before he grabbed a bush to stop his plunge.

"All right, Reid," Hatch barked. "That's enough!"

"Son of a bitch woulda killed me back there if he had the chance," Reid snapped.

"I don't blame him. I've thought about that myself."

"What's that supposed to mean?" Reid growled.

Hatch ignored the question. "Get up, Senator. And don't try anything else or I will let him kill you."

"All right," Williston gasped. Cut and bruised, Williston managed to pull himself to his feet. He stumbled the remaining way down the hill, the fight drained from him. When he reached the creek bed, he sat on a rock to rest.

Two saddled horses were tied next to Windwalker's ponies.

"Get some rope and tie his hands behind him," Hatch ordered.

Reid cut a length of rope from one of the pony's leads. Putting his rifle well out of reach, he approached Williston. "Get up!"

Williston wanted to say something smart-assed to his tormentor, but thought better of it. He stood compliantly.

"Turn around!"

Williston obeyed. Reid pulled the senator's hands behind his back. Wrapping the rope as tightly as possible around the wrists, Reid tied two strong knots. "That'll hold ya," Reid said with a chuckle. He pointed Williston in the direction of the ponies and shoved.

Williston stumbled toward the horses but did not fall. Hatch had led the horses from beneath the willow saplings.

"Put him on one of the Indian ponies," Hatch ordered as he climbed onto his own horse.

Reid was deceptively strong. He lifted Williston by his belt and hoisted him onto the back of the pony. *If I had known he could do that,* Williston thought, *I don't think I would have tangled with him.*

"What about the other horse?" Reid asked.

"Turn him loose. If anyone finds it, they'll think the old man fell off."

Reid shooed the other horse away. Taking the rope lead for Williston's pony, Reid climbed onto his own horse. The three men started down the canyon.

## 21

LANSING FOLLOWED THE HORSE TRACKS FOR NEARLY FIVE miles before losing the hoofprints to the rocky hills. He crouched close to the ground for a long time looking for the telltale scrape of a metal shoe against the stony ground. His horse followed obediently behind, his reins dragging on the ground.

It was almost noon when Lansing made his decision. "Okay, Cement Head. Let me run this one past you. The tracks look like they're headed that way." He pointed his finger in the direction of the highest hills in front of them. "We'll go in that direction for one hour. If we don't find anything, we'll turn around and head back for home."

Cement Head snorted and started to turn toward the desert they had just left. Lansing grabbed the reins. "Come on, old buddy. One hour. That's all I ask. I'd do the same for you." The sheriff swung himself into the saddle. "Besides, I know how badly you want to do this. You wouldn't forgive yourself if I caught the bad guys all by myself."

He gave Cement Head a nudge with his heels. The horse whinnied in protest, but started toward the high country anyway.

Lansing kept scanning the ground for any type of

trail. There was nothing to indicate anyone had passed that way recently. After forty-five minutes of wasted effort, the rider and mount found themselves at the rim of a canyon.

Lansing's inclination was to turn south. When he pulled the reins toward the right, Cement Head resisted. Lansing tugged on the reins harder and gave the horse a gentle kick in the sides. "I told you. Today it's my turn to be boss."

The horse reluctantly proceeded in the direction he was ordered. The two paralleled the canyon rim for five minutes when Lansing heard the distant sound of gunfire echoing through the canyons. The reports came from somewhere behind them. Cement Head whinnied.

"I don't want to hear it," Lansing snorted, turning his horse toward the north. "One lucky guess in ten years does not make you J. Edgar Hoover."

They headed north along the canyon rim. Once they were past the point where their trail had intersected the gorge, Lansing slowed the pace, searching for tracks and a path leading into the canyon. They had traced the lip of the canyon for nearly twenty minutes before Lansing found a trail leading down.

He got off his horse and looked at the ground along the path. Horses had definitely used the path. He could make out the distinct impressions of shoed horses. Beneath those tracks were the less defined prints of unshod ponies.

The sheriff and his horse had already started their descent into the canyon when the muffled sound of automatic rifle fire erupted. The blasts came from the direction they were headed. Lansing urged his horse to go a little faster, but Cement Head seemed to have his own opinion about how to handle the steep path. It was another five minutes before they reached the dry, sandy canyon floor.

The horse tracks were very easy to follow now. Cement Head picked up his pace.

As they rounded a bend in the canyon, three men on horseback approached from the opposite direction. When the man on the lead horse saw Lansing, he pulled the pistol from his holster and started firing.

Cement Head reared. Lansing grabbed his rifle from its saddle holster and jumped from the back of his horse. Cement Head turned and galloped back down the canyon. Lansing scrambled for the cover of a small outcropping of rocks.

Two of the men on horseback were now firing at Lansing. The third man was kicking his horse furiously, heading in the direction of the sheriff.

Williston wasn't paying much attention as he and his captors proceeded down the canyon. He tried to struggle with the ropes around his wrists, but the knots were too tight. He realized that the more he struggled, the more numb his hands became from lack of circulation.

His awareness was brought to the present when Hatch began firing his pistol. Fifty yards farther down the canyon there was another man on a horse. The man was dressed in a khaki uniform, and Williston thought he saw the flash of a badge. It was just for a second, though. The man's horse reared. A moment later the man was on the ground and diving for cover behind some rocks.

It was then that Williston realized Reid had dropped the rope to the pony and had joined Hatch in firing at the stranger. Williston didn't hesitate a moment. He began spurring his horse. "Come on, boy," the senator yelled above the gunfire.

The pony leapt past the other horses in a scramble to get away from the guns.

Williston kept his eyes on the spot where the

stranger had taken sanctuary. He told himself if he could make it that far he would be safe. Somewhere, lost in his subconscious mind, was the detached thought that you really could hear bullets when they whiz past you. The more relevant present took hold when his pony stumbled. His hands tied behind his back, Williston could do nothing but watch as the earth came crashing toward him.

Lansing's first thought was to eliminate the man charging him. He popped up from behind the rocks to take aim when he realized the man galloping toward him was unarmed. In fact, the man didn't have any arms showing.

Lansing ducked behind the rock again. He made a mental estimate of where the other assailants were. He rolled a few feet to his left, then popped up again. He began firing his rifle as rapidly as possible at the other two riders.

The pony the unarmed man was riding stumbled. Both horse and rider tumbled to the ground. This helped Lansing. It gave him a clearer view of the other men.

Whatever the intentions of the gunmen had been, they seemed to quickly change. As soon as the unarmed man fell, the other two turned their horses and headed down the canyon in the opposite direction. Lansing tried to get a parting shot at them, but they disappeared behind the bend in the canyon wall.

Sure that it was safe, Lansing abandoned his protective rocks to check on the fallen man.

Williston was conscious. He couldn't get up because the horse was lying on his leg. He saw the sheriff approaching. "I'd get up and thank you for saving me," Williston said, "but I seem to have a small problem here." He motioned toward the horse with his head.

"Let's see what we can do," Lansing replied, setting

his rifle against a rock. He grabbed the senator under the armpits. "Push with your other foot," Lansing instructed.

It took three pulls before Williston was free. He sat on the ground, rotating his foot to see if it still worked.

Lansing pulled out his hunting knife and started cutting the rope binding Williston's wrists. "Friends of yours?" Lansing gestured down the canyon.

"No." Williston shook his head. "As a matter of fact, we just met." The ropes fell from the senator's hands. Once free, he gently rubbed the rope burns on his wrists. "Thanks, Sheriff . . . ?"

"Lansing." The sheriff extended his hand to help the senator to his feet. "Cliff Lansing. San Phillipe County."

"Carter Williston," the senator said. It hurt for him to stand.

"*Senator* Carter Williston?"

Williston nodded.

Lansing took a closer look at the bruised, bleeding, and dirt-smeared face of the man he had just rescued. "I'll be a son of a gun. A couple of the gals who work at the diner said you were in town yesterday. I didn't believe them. . . ."

Lansing's tone was not fawning and he didn't appear to be impressed with who the senator was. Williston liked that.

Lansing knelt to check on the pony. The horse was breathing heavily. It had taken a bullet in the side and blood was oozing from its nostrils. Lansing pulled his pistol from its holster and shot the suffering animal in the head.

"Was that necessary?" Williston asked uncomfortably.

"She took a bullet in the lung," Lansing explained, holstering his gun. "She didn't need to suffer any longer." He walked over and picked up his rifle.

"Would you mind explaining to me what this was all about?"

"Sheriff, I wish I could. I don't know what the hell is going on."

"Okay," Lansing said thoughtfully. "Then maybe you can tell me why you are up here."

"I'm here at the request of the Zuni tribe and Joseph Windwalker— Damn!" Williston interrupted himself. "I've got to find Windwalker." He started up the canyon in the same direction the two gunmen had taken.

Lansing was mystified. "Who's Windwalker? What happened to him?"

"Those two bastards shot him. I need to find out if he's still alive."

Lansing looked down the canyon in the direction Cement Head had galloped. He shrugged in frustration. Under his breath he said, "I'll catch up with you later, horse."

## 22

LANSING QUICKLY CAUGHT UP WITH WILLISTON. "I THINK I'D better tag along, Senator, just in case your constituents show up again."

"I don't think those two voted for me." Williston found himself limping slightly.

"Do you know who they were?"

"I caught two names: Reid and Hatch. That's all I know."

Lansing thought for a moment. "The names don't ring a bell. We get a lot of transients, though. If they don't get in trouble, I don't hear about them." He noticed the senator's limp. "How far are we going?"

"Quarter of a mile, maybe."

Lansing kept his pace even with Williston's, in case the senator needed help walking. "You don't know what those two men wanted?"

"Hatch, evidently the smarter one of the two, said they wanted to talk to Windwalker."

"What about?"

"He wouldn't tell me. He said it was a private matter."

"You said you were up here because of the Zunis?"

"Have you heard anything about the land transfer between the federal government and the Zuni tribe?"

"Certainly. Has to do with the Anasazi Strip. Most of the Strip's in San Phillipe County. In fact, we're in the middle of it right now."

"Well, after a year of saying yes to the transfer, the tribal council is having second thoughts."

"Second thoughts? About what? Their reservation is almost two hundred miles from here." Lansing was puzzled. "I got the impression this was just a paperwork shuffle. Sign a new treaty and it's a done deal."

"So did I," Williston admitted. "Turns out there is one man opposed to the proposal. I was told if I could convince him the land swap was a good idea, the council would agree to it."

"Who's the one man blocking the deal?"

"Joseph Windwalker. The man we're trying to find."

"The one your two friends shot?"

"Yeah. That's the one." Williston saw the knot of willows. He searched the canyon wall for the entrance to the tunnel. It wasn't visible from the stream bed. He pointed in the general direction they would go. "Up there is a passageway leading to another canyon."

Lansing scanned the cliff face. "I don't see anything."

"It's well hidden. You won't even see it until you're on top of it."

They reached the bottom of the wash leading to the passage. Williston had to sit and rest before making the climb.

"You going to be all right?" Lansing asked.

"Yeah." Williston nodded. "I'll be fine."

"How'd you get so banged up? That wasn't just from the fall with the horse, was it?"

"I don't think so." Williston shook his head. "I made the mistake of trying to take on the big guy called Reid. I got my ass kicked." He thought about washing his face in the stagnant pool the ponies had watered from earlier. Then he remembered the cool, refreshing water at the cliff dwelling. He decided he could wait. "How'd you happen to come along when you did, Sheriff?"

"Three days ago a man was killed in the foothills about ten miles from here. I thought I had the shooter in jail. At the autopsy yesterday I found out the victim was probably shot by someone else. I decided I'd better come back for a closer look."

"If this guy was shot ten miles from here, what are you doing in this canyon?"

"I started off following a trail to a parked truck. Then I followed a trail *from* a parked truck. Then I lost the trail. Then I heard gunshots. Now I'm here. The men I was tracking could be the same ones who grabbed you."

"Sounds likely. I haven't seen anyone else up here. Did you lose their trail in the sandstorm?" He was thinking about the kiva and the sudden wind that had erupted.

"I don't know what you're talking about. There haven't been any sandstorms around here. There hasn't even been a breeze."

He gave the senator a quizzical look. "You were in a sandstorm?"

Williston nodded. "The next canyon over. 'Bout an hour ago, I guess."

"Okay." Lansing was doubtful but didn't argue. "Maybe it was a dust devil or something."

Williston caught the doubt in Lansing's tone. "Yeah. Maybe that's what it was." Williston knew what a sandstorm looked like. He'd seen hundreds as a kid growing up in Albuquerque. He knew that hadn't been a dust devil.

The senator stood. He could have rested a few more minutes, but he was anxious to find out what happened to Windwalker. He started up the wash toward the tunnel.

Lansing kept his distance behind Williston. He didn't want the senator to lose his footing and fall on him.

The entrance to the tunnel was just as Williston described. Lansing didn't see it until his guide disappeared through the opening. The sheriff hesitated before entering. There weren't a lot of things that bothered Lansing. Caves and mines bothered him. He took a deep breath, then plunged through the entrance.

"Are you still up there, Senator?" Lansing called into the dark.

"Yes," Williston called back. "The passage goes straight through. There's no way to get lost."

Lansing kept bumping against the walls in his haste to get through the tunnel. His eyes had not adjusted completely to the darkness by the time he emerged on the other side.

Williston watched Lansing's face when the sheriff saw the cliff dwelling for the first time.

"Damn!" the sheriff exclaimed, his eyes wide with the new discovery. "I had no idea there was anything like this in San Phillipe." He looked at Williston. "You didn't tell me about this."

"Sheriff, I didn't even think about it until we were almost here."

Williston limped toward the base of the canyon wall below the dwelling. He found Windwalker's hat where Reid had tossed it. Picking it up, he pointed to the small city above them. "We were up there. Hatch and Reid had their guns pointed at us. Before I knew what was happening, Windwalker knocked me back into the dwelling we had just left.

"He told me to climb into the upper apartments and pull the ladders up behind me. Then he disappeared. I don't know how long I was scrambling around up there. I worked my way through the interior rooms and ended up just above the toeholds cut into the rock. That's when Reid started shooting at Windwalker. I yelled at him to stop. When I looked back, Windwalker was gone."

"Did Windwalker get hit?"

"I don't know. I can't see how Reid could have missed at that range. I looked around the plaza but there was no sign of the Indian. Reid claims he jumped over the edge. All they found down here was Windwalker's hat." He held it up for Lansing to examine.

"Maybe Windwalker's still up there." Lansing pointed toward the dwellings. "How long did they look?"

"Five, ten minutes, maybe. Not very long. The not-so-bright one, Reid, thought he might have fallen on a ledge. Maybe we just can't see it from down here."

"I wouldn't rule that out. I read that the Anasazi always had an alternate way down in case of attack. Might be worth a look." He saw Williston eyeing the climb. "Think you can make it up?"

"No problem." Williston smiled. He tossed the hat aside and started scaling the wall.

Lansing started the climb, then realized he couldn't carry his rifle and grab the handholds at the same time. "Hey, Senator. How'd those two guys get their rifles up there?"

"Their guns had shoulder straps," Williston responded. "Is there a problem?"

"No," the sheriff replied. He leaned his rifle against the rock he was about to climb. He consoled himself with the thought they would only be up there a few minutes and that his gun would still be there when they climbed down. He followed Williston up the wall.

When they reached the level of the city, Williston asked Lansing if he was thirsty.

"I hadn't given it much thought," Lansing admitted, "but I could use something to drink."

Williston took him to the kitchen apartment the senator had first visited. The stone had not been replaced over the cistern. Williston filled the gourd with fresh water and offered it to the sheriff. While Lansing quenched his thirst, Williston scooped a bowlful of water from the well and washed his face, hands, and wrists. When that chore was done, the senator drank his fill of the cool, clear liquid.

Lansing was amazed at the pottery and other craft works distributed throughout the room.

"Every apartment dwelling in this complex has similar items. And everything is in mint condition."

"It's remarkable how well things stay preserved in the arid desert," Lansing commented, returning a bowl to a niche.

"I think there's more to the story than that," Williston observed. "It's not so much that it was preserved, but that it was left here to begin with. Whoever lived here had to leave in quite a hurry. Otherwise, they would have taken most of the stuff around here."

"Whatever the explanation, I think this Hatch and Reid are the ones I'm looking for."

"What makes you so sure?"

"Motive. The guy killed a few days ago had been digging in an old Indian village. His partner said they'd unearthed a couple of dozen pottery pieces intact. When I found the body, the relics were missing. Until this morning, I didn't think the relics actually existed. Then I found their digs."

"Why would that necessarily link Hatch and Reid?"

"Look around you, Senator. This is the richest archeological find in the history of this state.

"You always hear stories about lost Indian cities and hidden treasure. You don't necessarily want to discount them all. Here we are at the end of the twentieth century and there are still parts of the West that are unexplored.

"Those two jokers followed you and Windwalker here. At one time they may have intended to talk with the Indian, but only to find out what he knew about places like this. Why else were they in such a hurry to kill him? They found out what they wanted to know."

"That makes sense," Williston agreed. "I've learned in the last few days there's a lot of money to be made in Native American artifacts."

"Let's see if we can find out about Windwalker."

The two men stepped out the door onto the plaza. Williston showed the sheriff the approximate location where the gunmen stood. Lansing bent over and picked up an expended shell.

"What kind of guns did they have?"

"One was a Winchester of some type. The other was definitely an M-16."

"That's what this shell's for. Duke, the guy who was shot a couple days ago, was killed by a twenty-two, twenty-four caliber weapon. The caliber on an M-16 is twenty-two-three. Something like that." He dropped the shell casing into his pocket. "Looks like my case against these two guys is getting stronger." He picked up another casing. "This is for a thirty caliber carbine." He dropped the second shell into his pocket as well.

Williston then showed the lawman the general area where Windwalker had supposedly jumped from the ledge. Lansing leaned over the edge.

"I can't tell if there's anything down there." He held out his arm. "Hold on to me. Let me see if I can lean out a little farther."

"You sure about this?" Williston asked, grabbing Lansing's hand and wrist with both hands.

"No," Lansing confessed. "Just don't let go."

Lansing leaned out a little further. "A little bit more."

Williston let his feet scoot slightly closer to the edge. The sand-coated surface of the shelf did not give him a lot of traction.

"There is a ledge . . ." Lansing strained. "Six, maybe eight feet down. I can't tell how wide it is. . . . Pull me in."

Williston struggled to pull the sheriff toward him. His foot slipped on the loose surface and he fell to the ground, but he did not let go of Lansing. Sitting down, he had more leverage. He gave a monumental pull, heaving Lansing onto the ground next to him.

"You okay?" Williston asked.

"Yeah. Thanks," Lansing said. He was out of breath from the terror of the moment. "I didn't see any sign of your Indian friend."

"If he landed on that ledge, he's probably long gone by now."

"Well, we need to do the same thing," Lansing pointed out, getting to his feet. "It's going to take us a good four hours to walk out of this place. I'll have to come back tomorrow and see if I can find him."

Williston sighed. "Yeah, I suppose you're right." It was painful to stand. The bumps and bruises of the day were taking their toll.

The two men walked back to the stone ladder they had used to scale the rock face.

"You'd better let me go first," Williston suggested. "If my ankle decides to give out, you don't want me falling on you."

"Excellent suggestion," Lansing said in agreement.

Williston started down. He had descended only four feet when a piece of the rock face shattered next to his hand, followed a second later by the report of a gun.

Lansing had been paying too much attention to Williston's descent to notice Hatch and Reid emerging from the tunnel. He looked up at the sound of the rifle shot. Both men were aiming in his direction.

"Senator," Lansing shouted. "Get up here! Now!"

Williston started scrambling back up the stone wall. Gunfire was coming from both rifles now.

Lansing grabbed Williston's hand as soon as he was within reach and dragged him the rest of the way. Lansing kept pulling until both men were clear of the gunmen's sighting angle.

Lansing sat next to the prone senator. "You okay?"

"Yeah. Thanks," Williston said, catching his breath. Then he started laughing. "Didn't we have this same conversation five minutes ago?"

"Yeah," Lansing chuckled. "I think we did." His chuckle stopped. "Dammit!"

"What's wrong?"

"My rifle." Lansing looked toward the edge. "I left it at the bottom."

"I wouldn't suggest getting it right now."

"No," Lansing shook his head. "I guess not."

"What do we do now?"

"We'll have to wait. They're not going to storm our castle. Even if they do find my rifle down there, they'll suspect I still have a side arm. With only one way up, they won't try anything during daylight."

"What happens after dark?"

"We have plenty of daylight left to figure that one out."

"Why do you think they came back, Sheriff?"

"What do you think, Senator?"

"They left too many witnesses behind," Williston said grimly.

"That would be my guess too."

# 23

BETS WALKED INTO THE KITCHEN TO GRAB A COKE FROM THE refrigerator.

"How was the ride today, señorita?" Ramón asked as he chopped meat for a stew.

"It was hot, Ramón." She popped the tab on the cola and took a sip. "Is my father around?"

"*Sí.* Señor McGaffrey is in his study. He said he did not want to be disturbed."

"Good." Bets didn't want to find her father. She wanted to avoid him.

As she headed down the hallway of the sprawling ranch house she could hear her father thundering at someone. Normally she ignored his bellicose ways, but she heard Senator Williston's name mentioned. The door to the study was open, so she ventured a peek.

McGaffrey was on the phone, his back to the door. "I don't give a damn what Senator Williston told you, Harding. He's not going to be here tonight. He told me personally he would not be back till tomorrow night at the earliest. Probably not till Saturday . . .

"Yes, I guess you can construe that as a change of plans if you want. . . .

"No, Longtree didn't say anything about being in court tomorrow. Not to me anyway . . . I don't give a damn what his office said. For all I know he's on his way back to Santa Fe right now. . . .

"No. I don't have a way to get in touch with the senator. If you want to climb these mountains around here and find him, more power to you. . . .

"All right. I'll give him the message whenever he gets back here. . . ."

Bets hurried down the hall to her room before her father saw her.

As she undressed to take a shower she thought about her father's telephone call. It didn't jibe with the conversation she heard during breakfast. Senator Williston said he would be back late in the afternoon. She remembered that, because she was looking forward to having dinner with him. The lawyer, Longtree, had definitely said he had to get back to Santa Fe that night.

The clock on her dresser read four-thirty already.

Bets showered and put on clean clothing. Instead of her riding boots, she wore tennis shoes. Returning the empty cola can to the kitchen, she found Ramón still busy cooking.

"How many people for dinner tonight, Ramón?" Bets asked casually.

"Just you and Señor McGaffrey . . . and maybe Señor Parker if he gets back."

"What about Senator Williston?"

"No. No Senator Williston."

She thought about the morning conversation once more. It wasn't more than ten or fifteen minutes from the time she left the table until the senator and lawyer left. She couldn't understand how their plans changed so drastically in such a short amount of time.

Bets reached into the refrigerator and took out another cola. She popped the tab. "Oh, darn!"

"What's wrong, señorita?" Ramón hurried over. "You cut yourself?"

"No," Bets whimpered. "I broke a nail . . . and I don't have any nail polish."

"You want me to go to town?"

"No, that's all right. You're cooking. I can go myself. If my father asks where I am, you tell him. Okay?"

"Si, señorita. I'll tell him."

Bets grabbed her pocketbook and a set of keys from a hall table. Minutes later she was in her Jeep Islander, heading down the road.

# 24

WILLISTON EMERGED FROM THE APARTMENTS TUCKED against the back wall of the massive sandstone overhang. If there had been an escape route built into the dwellings, he couldn't find it. He even tried squeezing into the water system, but there wasn't enough room.

Lansing had remained behind to guard the access to the cliff. Williston found him quietly building a stone wall at the top of the stone ladder.

"What's this?" Williston asked. He tried to keep his voice not much more than a loud whisper. "A barricade?"

"Not exactly." Lansing kept his head low as he stacked more stones on the wall. "Find anything?"

"Nothing." Williston sat wearily. He was worn out from the stooping and climbing through the maze of apartments. He watched Lansing's industry for a few more minutes. The wall was four feet long and two feet high. Finally he had to ask, "What the hell are you doing?"

"I haven't seen our friends for some time," Lansing explained, sitting next to the senator. "They're not around the tunnel entrance. I figure they're either looking for another way up or waiting at the bottom for us."

"You don't think they left, do you?"

Lansing gave the senator a look of exasperation.

"Wishful thinking," Williston apologized.

"I don't think those two have enough initiative to find a different way up here. So they're probably waiting right below us. I'm going to test my theory."

Williston eyed the wall and then his companion. "How?"

"If I can get you to help me, we're going to start a little avalanche."

Lansing sat behind his miniwall with his feet on the broad, flat stones he used for the foundation. He had Williston sit next to him. Together they pushed the base of the wall closer to the edge. "On the count of three," Lansing instructed. "One . . . two . . . three!"

Both men pushed the stack of rocks as hard as they could. The wall toppled over the side, the stones clacking and thumping as they tumbled to the canyon floor.

"Hey, look out!" Reid yelled.

"Get out of the way, you ass!" Hatch screamed.

Williston and Lansing listened for the last of the rocks thump to the bottom, then started laughing.

"You bastards," Reid bellowed from below. A storm of bullets came screaming from the M-16 toward the men on the cliff.

The lawman and the politician scooted further out of range. The bullets ricocheted harmlessly off the stone roof.

"I think he's pissed," Williston said with a laugh.

"I think you're right," Lansing agreed.

"I guess they *were* waiting for us down there," Williston observed. "Now what?"

"Build another wall."

"What good will that do? They wouldn't be stupid enough to sit in the same place again."

"True, but if they see it from below they'll have second thoughts about coming up that cliff face after dark." Lansing started walking toward the apartment buildings. "There's a stack of loose stones back here. When we're finished we can get some rest. It could be a long night."

## 25

MARGARITE CARERRA SAT AT A TABLE NEAR THE FRONT OF the diner. She wanted to make sure she wouldn't miss Lansing when he arrived. That was at five o'clock. Kelly asked her three times if she wanted to order. Three times the doctor told the waitress she was waiting for someone.

At five-fifteen Margarite was becoming worried something had happened to the sheriff. By five-thirty she had talked herself out of being worried. Now she was pissed at being stood up.

Kelly approached a fourth time to take her order. Margarite did not say a thing. She simply stood and stomped out of the diner.

Waitresses and patrons alike could hear the door to Dr. Carerra's truck slam shut. From their positions behind the counter, Velma and Kelly watched as Dr. Carerra backed her truck into the street without looking. Two cars skidded to a stop attempting to avoid hitting the doctor. Carerra was oblivious. She shifted into drive and squealed her tires as she sped north out of town.

"My, my." Velma tsked. "Did you see the way she took off? She almost killed two people out there. You'd think someone who took the Oath of Pythagoras would have a higher regard for human life."

"I think you meant the Hypocratic Oath," a customer at the counter commented.

"Don't you correct me," Velma snapped. "I date a doctor."

Kelly tapped Velma on the shoulder and pointed her attention toward the street. There was another squeal of tires as Dr. Carerra's truck came careening back down the street. She took the corner at the town square on two wheels, then gunned her engine all the way to the courthouse parking lot. The truck came to a screeching halt next to a squad car.

"Think she's pissed about somethin'?" Velma asked.

"From what I heard, she and Cliff were supposed to go out tonight. Looks like he didn't show up."

"Well, do you blame him?" Velma huffed. "The woman has an attitude."

Dr. Carerra stormed into the reception area of the sheriff's office. Deputy Larry Peters sat at the spot Marilyn managed during the day. The deputy removed the telephone receiver from his ear. "Can I help you, ma'am?"

"Yes. I want to see the sheriff," the doctor demanded. "You can tell him Dr. Carerra is here."

"I'm sorry, ma'am, but Sheriff Lansing isn't back. . . . And I'm not supposed to be here yet. . . . Excuse me. . . ." He spoke into the phone. "Momma, can I call you back? I have someone here who needs to talk to the sheriff. . . . Yes, Momma, I told her the sheriff's not in. . . . Yes, Momma, it is a woman. . . . No, Momma, I don't know her. . . . Yes, that's a dear. I'll call you right back. . . . Yes, I love you too." He hung up the phone. Peters's speech style wasn't exactly slow. He referred to it as "precise." It was also very monotone.

"Now, can I help you, ma'am?"

"Well," Carerra said, calming down a bit, "I was supposed to meet the sheriff half an hour ago. I thought maybe he forgot."

"He's not back yet, ma'am. That's not to say he didn't forget to meet you, because he still could have. And I don't know how to reach him. You see, I just came in myself. I'm not supposed to come in until ten o'clock, but Marilyn had to leave. Then Stu Ortega had to take some samples to the crime lab in Santa Fe this morning but he's not back yet. And I know the sheriff told him to come straight back after dropping the samples off. Otherwise, he'd be holding down this shift till I came in at ten. And Joe Cortez. The other deputy on day shift? He has the sheriff's Jeep 'cause Joe's radio doesn't work in his patrol car. So he's off at Artesia 'cause somebody was in a fight or something and he didn't think he'd get back till later."

Carerra was numb from the deputy's dissertation. She was afraid of what might happen if she *asked* him a question. She chose her words carefully. "Do you know when the sheriff will be back?"

"No," came the one-word reply. Dr. Carerra was relieved.

A young woman entered the reception area from the outer door. She acted a bit reluctant as she approached the reception desk. "Excuse me," she apologized. "Am I interrupting?"

"Not at all," the doctor insisted. "Go ahead."

The girl turned to Peters. "I was wondering if I could talk to the sheriff?"

"The sheriff's not back yet," the deputy explained. "And the other deputies are out. But I'm in. So maybe I can help." He stood and extended his hand over the counter. "I'm Deputy Larry Peters."

The young lady gave the deputy's hand a curt shake. "I'm Bets . . . Elizabeth McGaffrey."

"Oh." The deputy smiled. "I'll bet you're related to Mack McGaffrey."

"He's my father," she admitted quietly.

"What can I do for you?" Peters asked, sitting back down.

"It's about Senator Williston. . . ."

"Senator Carter Williston? The U.S. senator?"

Bets nodded.

"You *know* Senator Williston?" The deputy sounded impressed.

"Yes, I do," Bets replied, getting tired of the deputy's tedious manner. "And I think he's in trouble."

"My, my." The deputy pondered the statement. "Why do you think he's in trouble?"

Bets tried to explain as quickly and simply as possible. "He spent last night at my father's ranch. He went with a lawyer this morning to talk to some old Indian down at the Anasazi Strip. He said he would be back this afternoon. But I heard my father telling someone on the phone he wouldn't be back until tomorrow or the next day."

The deputy looked at Carerra. "I didn't know the senator was in town. Did you?"

"I heard someone talking about it yesterday." Carerra nodded. She turned to Bets. "What kind of trouble do you think he's in?"

"I don't know. It's just this feeling I have, like something's not right."

"Ohh," the deputy said knowingly. "One of those."

Bets ignored him. "It doesn't make sense. This morning he said he would be back today. All of a sudden, he won't be back for two days."

"Did you ask your father about it?" Carerra asked.

"No," Bets replied defiantly. "He'd be the last one I'd ask."

Carerra studied the young lady standing in front of her. The doctor considered herself a pretty good judge of character. To her, the McGaffrey girl seemed sincere and very upset.

"I'll tell you what, miss," the deputy said, setting a pencil and a pad of paper on the countertop. "You sit at that table over there and write everything down on that tablet. I'll make sure the sheriff gets it as soon as he comes in."

"Isn't there some way you can send someone out there?"

"I'm afraid not." The deputy shook his head. "I'm waiting for one deputy to get back from Santa Fe. The other deputy is in Artesia and won't get back until late. I can't get in touch with the sheriff because he doesn't have a radio. And I can't leave my post."

"Do you know where on the Anasazi Strip Senator Williston went?" Carerra asked.

"South of town. I don't know exactly where."

"Sheriff Lansing went to the Strip today too. He was going south of town. We could drive down that way. Maybe we'll run into someone." She looked at the county map on the wall. "Deputy, do you know how Sheriff Lansing got to the Strip this morning?"

Peters came around the corner of the counter. "There are only a couple of good roads that go back that way." He pointed on the map. "There's one ten miles south and another about fifteen miles."

"But do you know which one the sheriff took?"

"The one fifteen miles south?" the deputy guessed.

"I guess we'll go find out." The doctor put her hand on Bets's shoulder and guided her to the door. "Elizabeth, my name is Margarite."

"Nice to meet you, Margarite." Bets smiled as they left the room. "But why are you doing this?"

"I'm a doctor," she explained. "It's my job to help people." *Besides,* she thought, *I just got stood up on my first date in six months. I want to find out why.*

## 26

WILLISTON LAY ON HIS BACK, EYES CLOSED, HIS HEAD CUPPED in his hands. Lansing sat a few feet away, leaning against a building, watching the access to the shelf.

"You have any kids, Sheriff?"

Lansing was startled at the question. "I thought you were asleep."

"I drifted off for a while," Williston responded, not opening his eyes. "Anyway, you have any kids?"

"I have a son. Cliff junior. We call him C.J. He's twelve. Lives with his mom down in Albuquerque."

"Divorced?"

"Yeah." There was true disappointment in his voice.

Williston looked up. "Sorry."

"It's not bad. I get to see him a couple of times a month and he stays with me for four weeks during the summer."

"What happened, if you don't mind my asking?"

"When all else fails, the lawyers fall back on 'irreconcilable differences.' I was on the Albuquerque police force for about ten years. That's where I met Pam, in Albuquerque. I didn't care much for the big city. When I had the chance to come back to Las Palmas as chief deputy, I grabbed it.

"Never did ask her what she wanted. I just assumed

she'd love my hometown the way I do. I'll give her credit. She tried it for six months, but she wasn't cut out to live in a small town. She went back to Albuquerque. I stayed."

"And you wouldn't move to Albuquerque. Not even for the sake of your son?"

"It wouldn't be much of a life for him if I did. I'd be miserable and that would make his life miserable. Besides, his mom has a career. New friends. Except for C.J., I don't think we have much in common anymore."

Williston sat up. The shadows were growing longer in the canyon. His watch said five-thirty. "How much longer until dark?"

"Three, three and a half hours . . . You have any kids?"

Williston shook his head. "No. Just wasn't in the cards."

"You want to take a spell at this? I think I'll close my eyes for a while."

"Sure."

Lansing handed the senator his pistol. The sheriff could tell he found the gun heavy. "It's a three-fifty-seven Magnum. On the rare occasions when I have to use it, I know I'll stop what I'm aiming at."

With his hat tipped over his face, Lansing assumed the pose Williston used minutes earlier. "After thirty years in the navy, why'd you want to get into politics?" Lansing asked.

"There are politics in every line of work, Sheriff. It's just not always called that.

"I spent a lot of years at the Pentagon. As influential as the military seemed to be, the real power was across the Potomac. I've seen a four-star admiral with thirty-five years of service get reamed by a freshman congressman. I danced around the fringes of power for a long time. When the opportunity came that I could be a part of the inner circle, I jumped at it."

"Ego?" Lansing asked.

"I lied to myself for a while about that. I told myself I wanted to make a difference. But, yeah, it was ego. I got a kick out of chewing on the same navy brass that chose not to promote me. I also found out a junior senator from New Mexico controls one percent of the votes in the Senate, and that's about it. Most of the time, he doesn't even control that much."

"Is it worth it?"

"Politics? You mean, did I have to pay a price for where I am today?" Williston shrugged. "You tell me. You had to be elected to become sheriff."

"Yeah," Lansing admitted. "I did. But my politics are on a very small scale. The election was a means to an end. See, I'm in law enforcement. I'd be doing that whether or not I got elected sheriff."

"In politics, in life, in a pursuit of a career, every man has his price, Sheriff."

"I don't think that's necessarily true," Lansing countered.

"You had yours," Williston pointed out. "You gave up your family so you could stay here in the sheriff's department."

Lansing defended himself. "There were other things behind the divorce. Not just my career choice."

"But you're doing what you wanted to do and you had to give up something to have it. That's paying a price, Sheriff, no matter which way you cut it."

Lansing mulled over Williston's observation. Maybe he had paid a price for where he was, but he had never thought of his life in those terms. He considered asking the senator, What was your price for getting into Congress? The thought passed. He wasn't sure he wanted to know. Williston never did answer the question "Is it worth it?"

# 27

ROUTE 15 SOUTH OF TOWN WAS NEARLY DESERTED. IT WAS dinnertime and the locals who normally used the highway were home eating. It was difficult to talk in Bets McGaffrey's Jeep with the top removed. Both women had to yell to be heard, so the conversation was kept to a minimum. The noise in the open Jeep was compounded by the fact that Bets was driving twenty-five miles per hour over the speed limit. She felt secure in the thought that the sheriff and all his deputies were nowhere to be found. If they were nearby, she explained to Dr. Carerra, this would be the quickest way to find them.

Several gravel roads intersected the highway. Most, however, were privately owned and led to the small ranches and farms that made up the majority of San Phillipe County. Deputy Peters had pointed to two roads that led directly to the Anasazi Strip. The first was ten miles south of town. Bets slowed her Jeep as they neared the junction.

"That's the ten-mile road," she said to Carerra. "What do you think?"

The doctor surveyed the hills quickly. She saw no vehicles and no dust being churned up indicating a vehicle was approaching. She shook her head. "Let's keep going. I don't see a thing."

Bets agreed. "The deputy said it would be the next one, anyway." She stepped on the accelerator and within a few seconds had reached eighty again.

From the highway, the road at the fifteen-mile point didn't look any more promising. With their choice of options decreasing, they decided to follow it.

Off the highway, Bets had to slow down considerably. That gave Dr. Carerra a chance to talk with her. "Why wouldn't you ask your father about Senator Williston?"

"Because . . ." She hesitated. "Because we just don't talk."

"Could you have asked your mother?" Carerra probed.

"My mother's dead!" Bets snapped. San Phillipe and Las Palmas were so small, she assumed everyone knew about the McGaffrey tragedy.

"I'm sorry," Carerra apologized. "I didn't know."

"I guess you're not from around here."

"No, I'm not."

"I'm the one who should apologize. My mother's been dead for a long time. . . ." She gave her next statement a great deal of consideration before expressing it. "I didn't ask my father about Senator Williston . . . because I know I can't trust him. I can't trust a damned thing he says. I don't think anyone should."

Dr. Carerra thought about the statement. There was a lot more emotion behind the words than an adolescent's disdain for adults in general and a parent in particular. "Elizabeth, is there always friction between you and your father?"

"Very little. We hardly see each other. I've been in boarding schools ever since I was ten," Bets explained. "I come back to the ranch every summer, but my father spends most of his time away. He has his business and his mistresses. . . . That works out fine for me."

"Slow down a minute," Carerra instructed. She studied a pear cactus plant as they passed it. "Did you notice that cactus?"

"No, not really."

"There's another one up ahead," the doctor said, pointing down the dirt road. "Stop just before we get there."

Bets obeyed. Shutting off her engine, they got out of the Jeep to examine the plant.

"See how the branches have been torn away?" Kneeling, Dr. Carerra gingerly picked up a broken "pear" by its long needle. "On the plant, you can see where the juice is still oozing. Somebody did drive down this road today. It's been a few hours, though. You can tell by the way the plant has almost sealed its skin where the branch was broken off."

"What are you? A botanist?" Bets asked, examining the plant.

"No." Carerra smiled. "I'm a medical doctor. What I know about cacti is from a lifetime of living around the desert." She tossed the cactus aside. "At least we know we're on somebody's trail. Let's get going."

As they drove deeper into the foothills they passed an occasional track that veered into more rugged terrain. They chose to stay on what passed for a road.

It was nearly seven o'clock when they rolled into a large, flat area nestled in the hills. At the end of the small valley was an adobe shack. Next to the shack was a beat-up looking Jeep.

"That's Mr. Longtree's car!" Bets exclaimed.

"Who's Mr. Longtree?"

"He's the lawyer I told you about. The one with Senator Williston." Bets pulled her Jeep alongside the parked vehicle. Shutting off the engine, she jumped from the car.

"Senator Williston?" she called, walking toward the shack. "Mr. Longtree?" No one responded.

Dr. Carerra climbed from her seat. She stood next to the Jeep as Bets looked for the two men.

The door to the hut was closed. Bets tapped on the wood and called, "Hello? Is anyone in there?" With no response coming from inside, she pushed the door open.

The lengthening shadows from the surrounding hills had enveloped the small building. The one-room interior was nearly dark. As the girl's eyes adjusted to the dim light, she saw the form of a man seated along the far wall.

"Mr. Longtree?"

The shape didn't respond.

Bets approached closer. "Mr. Longtree, is that you?" She bent to get a better look.

Dr. Carerra was peering inside Longtree's Jeep when she heard the scream. Running to the shack, she collided with the McGaffrey girl in the doorway.

"Elizabeth," Carerra said, grabbing the young lady. "What's wrong?"

Bets was nearly in hysterics. "M-Mr. Longtree! He's dead!"

Carerra released the girl and rushed inside. It took her a moment to discern shapes. She saw Longtree sitting across the room. There was no movement.

Approaching the man, she knelt a few feet away. Longtree sat with his back against the wall. His eyes bulged from their sockets and his face was awash in sheer terror. His throat had been sliced open.

As she examined the corpse more closely, the doctor could tell the gash was so deep it reached the spinal column. The blood-stained shirt had been ripped open. A jagged incision had been made through the sternum that continued to the navel.

Carerra carefully inspected the chest wound. Her

fingers were covered with blood by the time she discovered the heart had been removed. On the floor next to the body was a stone-bladed knife with a bone handle. The knife was crusted with dried blood.

The doctor emerged from the hut. Bets was leaning against her Jeep, her face buried in her hands, sobbing.

"Elizabeth!"

"What?" she whimpered.

"Check and see if there's any gas in Longtree's spare can."

"What for?" Bets asked, trying to regain her composure.

"I need to wash my hands," Carerra explained, quietly but firmly. "That's the closest thing we have to a disinfectant right now."

Wiping her eyes, Bets unstrapped the five-gallon can from the rear of Longtree's Jeep. A little fluid sloshed inside. Bets removed the cap and sniffed. "It's gasoline," she confirmed.

"Good. Bring it over here." Dr. Carerra distanced herself ten feet from the vehicles. "Pour a little at a time."

The doctor scrubbed the blood from her hands as Bets splashed the gas out a little at a time. "Twenty years ago health-care workers didn't have to worry about getting a little blood on them," the doctor explained. "Nowadays we get paranoid at the sight of it. . . . That's good."

Bets quit pouring and put the lid back on the can.

Carerra used a handful of loose dirt to scrub her hands. The dirt dried her hands and absorbed much of the gasoline odor. In the back of Longtree's Jeep was a plastic jug full of water. She used the water sparingly to clean her hands a little more. She took a sip of the water, then handed the jug to Bets.

"Here," the doctor insisted. "Drink some of this."

Bets did as she was told.

"Looks like you were right, Elizabeth. Something is going on. . . ." Carerra looked at the surrounding hills. "We need to get back to town."

"Town? What about Senator Williston?"

"What about Senator Williston?"

"He's in trouble. We need to help him!"

"Elizabeth, there's not a damned thing we can do for him right now. It's going to be dark in less than two hours. Whoever killed Longtree is still out here somewhere. If they haven't killed the senator already, I don't know what we could do to stop them. We need to report this to the authorities."

"You mean Deputy Larry back in Las Palmas? He can't leave his post!"

"Maybe Sheriff Lansing will be back by the time we get there. All I know is we can't stay here."

Bets nodded. She knew the doctor was right. They couldn't stay there. "All right," she agreed. She looked at the shack. "What about Mr. Longtree?"

"We'll close the door. Maybe that will keep the animals out. We don't want to disturb anything until the sheriff gets here."

Carerra pulled the door closed. Finding a stick on the ground, she used it as a wedge to hold the door tightly shut. When she finished, she found Bets waiting for her in her Jeep.

"Let's go," Carerra said, climbing in.

Bets shifted into reverse. Swinging the vehicle around, she was pointed down the road when a metallic thunk sounded at the front of the Jeep. A split second later a rifle report echoed through the hills.

Steam started pouring from the radiator. The second rifle shot shattered the windshield, the bullet whizzing between the driver and passenger.

Carerra used all her strength to push Bets from the moving Jeep. As the girl tumbled out, the doctor dove out the opposite side. The Jeep sputtered ahead a few feet as a third bullet smashed through the windshield and embedded in the passenger seat.

Carerra rolled once when she hit the ground, then was on her feet. A second later she had the stunned Elizabeth by the hand and the two were running for the protection of the shack.

Margarite bypassed the door, heading for the back of the building. She had no intention of being trapped inside.

"You all right?" the doctor asked, peering around the corner to see if they were being chased yet.

"Yes," Bets gasped. "Who is shooting at us?"

"Whoever killed Longtree." It looked like the coast was clear for the moment. "Wait here!"

Carerra ran from the protection of the building to Longtree's Jeep. As she suspected, there were no keys in the ignition. She grabbed the plastic water jug from the back floor as another rifle shot sounded. Carerra didn't stop to find out how close the bullet came. She scrambled for the cover of the building.

"What's that for?" Bets asked, seeing the jug. Her eyes were wild with panic.

"There are no keys in the other Jeep. We're going to have to walk out of here." The doctor tried to sound as calm as possible. "We won't go far without water."

Behind the shack was the arroyo descending from the mountains. "Let's go. Whoever's shooting at us must know we don't have any weapons. They'll be here any second." Carerra took a few steps toward the rocky wash. Bets hesitated, nearly paralyzed with fear.

"Come on, Elizabeth," Carerra said firmly. "We can't help anyone if we stay here and get killed." She held out her hand to the younger woman.

Bets looked from the proffered hand to the doctor's face, then nodded. "You're right," she admitted. She grasped Carerra's hand and stood. "Let's go."

# 28

AT THE TOP OF THE ARROYO THE TWO WOMEN FOUND A CLEAR path that would take them farther into the mountains. Carerra looked behind them. If anyone was following them, they weren't within sight yet.

Carerra decided to use the path. It may have been the most obvious route for them to follow, but she was more interested in putting distance between them and the shooter. Getting off the path would slow them down.

The trail exposed them along the top of a ridge. Out in the open like that, Carerra insisted they keep up their pace. Both women were in good shape. They kept a steady jog as the path descended into a canyon.

Carerra couldn't help but notice that Bets kept an anxious eye on the trail behind them. The doctor was sure that physical exertion was the only thing that kept her new friend from hysterics.

Neither had any idea how far or how long they had gone when Carerra called for a rest. They were on the canyon floor and the setting sun made the gorge seem even darker. To escape being viewed from above, Carerra picked a spot behind a boulder. Once they were settled, she opened the jug and took a gulp of water. She handed the jug to Bets, who did the same.

"What time is it?" Bets asked, nervously studying the canyon rim above them.

Margarite looked at her watch. "Seven-thirty . . . How are you doing?"

"Okay," Bets lied, still catching her breath. "Do you think they're following us?"

At the moment, Carerra didn't think an honest answer was wise. "I haven't seen any signs we're being followed. Maybe they lost our trail." She stood, screwing the lid back onto the water bottle. "But as long as it's daylight, we need to keep moving. Are you ready?"

"Sure. You want me to carry the jug for a while?"

"It would help." The two started down the canyon, their pace a bit slower than before.

After twenty minutes the path started leading out of the canyon. Carerra suggested they follow it. They could get boxed in with no way out if they stayed on the canyon floor. Bets had no argument with that. They stopped again for a rest once they reached the canyon rim. It was almost dark.

"I can't figure out why they want to kill us," Dr. Carerra confessed after taking a drink of water.

"Because we found a dead body!" There was an edge of desperation in Bets's voice. "They don't want anyone to know Mr. Longtree was killed."

"That's just it. Somebody did want the body found. . . . I didn't tell you this before, mostly because it didn't make a difference. . . . Whoever killed that man back there didn't just slit his throat. They cut out his heart."

"Oh, my God!" Bets whimpered, putting her hand over her mouth. "W-why?"

"I don't know. He was either killed as part of a ceremony, or it was staged to look like a ritual killing. There was a stone knife on the floor next to the body. The killer left the body and the knife there so they'd be found."

"Maybe they changed their mind. Maybe they didn't want the body found after all."

"Yeah," Carerra agreed. "Or maybe they were going to move the body . . . or maybe they wanted him found, just not yet and not by us. . . . Whatever is going on, we were at the wrong place at the wrong time."

"Do you think they were just trying to scare us?" Bets asked hopefully.

"That wouldn't make any sense. After finding the body we were already scared. They had to know we would go straight to the sheriff. They didn't want that to happen."

Bets suddenly looked around. She had an air of dazed confusion. "What direction are we going?"

"North," Carerra said confidently. "The sun set to our left. It's clear tonight, so we'll be able to use the North Star. We should have a full moon too. I think we've been moving in the general direction of Las Palmas. Can you remember how far we drove?"

Bets shrugged. "Fifteen miles by highway. I guess another ten by dirt road."

"That puts us around twenty, twenty-five miles from town. We can cover that distance by morning."

"What about cutting back to the highway?"

"Not yet, Elizabeth. Let's get a little farther north. I don't want to end up anywhere close to that dirt road we took."

"I guess that makes sense," Bets agreed. There was still an edge of desperation in her tone.

As the two women stood and started down the trail once more, Carerra tried to take the young woman's mind off the situation. "What are you, Elizabeth? Seventeen? Eighteen?"

"Seventeen . . . I just graduated from high school . . . from the Hampton Academy back East." The question seemed to calm her a little. "Margarite, if you'd like, you can call me Bets. That's what all my friends call me."

Carerra looked at her companion. "I hope you're not offended, but . . . Bets sounds like a good name for a little girl. That doesn't seem to fit the woman I've been dealing with the last few hours. I'd like to stick with 'Elizabeth,' if you don't mind."

"No." Bets smiled. "Elizabeth's fine. . . . In fact, I think I prefer it." There was a definite change in Bets's voice. She sounded more confident and a lot less anxious.

"Any plans for college?" Carerra asked, keeping up the distraction.

"Sure," Elizabeth confided. "I wanted to come back to New Mexico for school. But most of my friends from the academy are going to Smith College. If I came here, I wouldn't know anyone."

"You wouldn't have any trouble making new friends," Carerra said reassuringly. "Have you decided on a career?"

"I want to be a veterinarian . . . so I suppose it really doesn't matter where I get my B.A. I could go to the University of New Mexico veterinary school after Smith. The only drawback would be I'd be too close to my father."

The two walked along in silence for a while. Finally, Carerra had to ask: "Why do you hate your father so much?"

Elizabeth had been expecting the question. For the first time in her life she was ready to answer. "He killed my mother."

"What?" There was disbelief in the doctor's voice.

"When I was ten. There had been a party at their house in Santa Fe. My father had the poor taste to invite one of his mistresses.

"It was after midnight when I heard my folks arguing. It woke me up. It seemed like they argued all the time." Elizabeth stopped walking. She stared at the sparkling stars in the sky. "I covered my ears with my pillow so I couldn't hear the shouting. The pillow couldn't block out the gunshot. After that, the arguing stopped.

"I was scared, but got out of bed anyway. The house was dark, except for the light coming from my parents' room. The door was open just a little. . . . My mother was on the floor . . . a pool of blood . . . My father was kneeling next to her. He was putting the gun in her hand. . . ."

In the growing moonlight Dr. Carerra could see the tears streaming down Elizabeth's face. The irony of the picture was that the young woman's voice remained firm. "The police called it a suicide. My father said he was asleep downstairs when it happened. I told them I was asleep."

"You've never told anyone this story, have you?"

Elizabeth shook her head. "No."

"Why not?"

"No one would have believed me. Even if someone had, Mack McGaffrey would have bought his way out."

"Why are you telling me this now?"

"Because if something happens to me, I want the world to know what a bastard my father really is."

Carerra put her arm around the young woman. "Nothing's going to happen to you. Nothing's going to happen to either one of us." Somewhere ahead of them on the trail came a sound.

"Shh!" Carerra said, pulling the girl to the ground.

The noise came again. It was the clop of a hoof on rock and the tinkle of metal on metal.

"It's a horse," Elizabeth whispered.

The two looked in the direction of the sound. A hundred feet away, following the trail along the rim of the canyon, was a riderless horse.

"I think we just found some transportation," Carerra said, brushing herself off as she got up.

The animal stopped and watched as the women approached.

"Hey, boy," Elizabeth said soothingly as she reached out to grab the reins. The horse neighed softly but didn't try to pull away. He sniffed at the jug of water Bets was carrying. "Thirsty, huh?" She handed the water bottle to Carerra. "He needs something to drink. Pour the water into my cupped hands."

The doctor did as she was instructed, pouring until the jug was empty. The horse gratefully lapped the water as it sloshed into Elizabeth's hands and whinnied in protest when Carerra put the lid back on the bottle.

"Sorry," Elizabeth explained. "It's all gone."

The animal neighed argumentatively. Pulling the reins from the girl's grasp, he motioned with his head toward the saddle on his back. Elizabeth laughed as she pulled the canteen from the saddle horn. "No, I guess it's not all gone."

The two women repeated the procedure again, leaving some water in the canteen for themselves.

"I wonder where his rider is?" Elizabeth pondered, caressing the horse's neck.

"Or who?" The doctor speculated. She walked to the saddle bags and opened them. On one side were plastic zipper bags and rifle cartridges. Inside the other bag were foil-wrapped cakes of dried food, the kind used by campers and hikers.

"Hungry?" Carerra asked.

"Yeah," Elizabeth admitted. "Starving."

Carerra handed her a bar. "Looks like granola for dinner."

"Horse oats would taste good right now." Bets eagerly peeled the foil back and began eating.

Carerra checked the canteen. "We need to go easy

on the food. You're supposed to drink a pint of fluid for each bar. We don't have that much water left."

"This will be plenty." When Elizabeth finished the food bar she wadded the foil and stuffed it back in the saddle bag. "Don't want to leave a trail of garbage," she explained. She then lifted the stirrup to get a closer look at the saddle. Embossed on the leather was the name of the owner. The moon had just crept above the horizon, giving her enough light to discern the inscription. "Looks like it says 'Clifford A. Lansing, Las Palmas, New Mexico.' "

The doctor came for a closer look. "This is the sheriff's horse!"

"Oh, my God! What are we going to do?"

"We're going to borrow him and get to town as fast as we can."

"Do you think something's happened to the sheriff too?"

"I can't imagine he decided he'd rather walk. . . . Are you pretty good at riding?"

"Yes," Elizabeth said confidently.

"Good. You drive."

The McGaffrey girl climbed into the saddle. A moment later Carerra was seated behind her.

"Which way?" Elizabeth asked.

"Any way but the way we came."

Elizabeth pointed the horse north.

# 29

"WHAT DO YOU THINK?" THE SENATOR ASKED. "IS IT DARK enough yet?"

Lansing looked at the sky. There was barely a hint of fading sunlight. The bottom of the canyon was nearly black. "It's about as good as we're going to get," Lansing observed. "If we wait too much longer the moon will be out. Let's go for it."

They had to work from memory. They knew approximately where they had seen the ledge earlier in the day. Because Hatch and Reid were watching from below, they hadn't risked peering over the edge of the rock shelf since their first look.

As they knelt along the edge, Lansing took off his hat and bent forward. "I can't see a damned thing right now," he said in low tones. "I'm going to turn around and slide backward on my belly. I wish I had something to hold on to."

"Why don't we use your holster belt? I'll hold one end. I don't think I'll be able to pull you up if something goes wrong, but it will slow your slide a little."

"It's worth a try," the sheriff agreed. He removed the holster. Slipping his gun under his pants belt, behind his back, he handed Williston one end. Taking the other end of the belt, Lansing lay flat on his stomach and scooted backward over the edge.

The progress seemed painstakingly slow. Lansing could feel the beads of sweat popping out on his forehead. He knew gravity would take over any moment. When it did, he wasn't sure how far a drop to expect.

He felt himself starting to slide backward. Instinct told him to scramble back up the rock, but that would have defeated his goal. He held on tightly to the belt, his right arm stretched above his head. He held his breath as, suddenly, his feet touched the ledge below him.

He looked down. The ledge was two feet wide where he stood. To his left, in the direction of the rock ladder they had climbed earlier, the ledge abruptly ended only three feet away. To his right the ledge continued a good distance farther, disappearing into the darkness.

Lansing looked up. His head was barely below the rock ledge of the cliff dwellings. "I made it, Senator. The ledge is only six, six and a half feet down. Let me move down a little."

Still facing the rock wall, Lansing carefully sidestepped along the ledge, giving Williston an additional three feet of landing space.

"I'm letting go of the belt," Williston said.

"Got it!"

Williston rolled onto his stomach. He began pushing himself backward with his hands as he scooted closer to the edge. As with Lansing, gravity took over, pulling the senator onto the ledge. The sheriff put a reassuring hand on Williston's back to steady him.

"That was it?" Williston asked, finally opening his eyes.

"That was it," Lansing confirmed. "Let's get going."

With his back to the canyon, Lansing started sliding his feet along the ledge. In the darkness he couldn't tell how much progress he was making or how far he had to go. Williston followed the sheriff's lead, keeping a four-foot space between them.

"Damn," Lansing muttered.

"What's wrong?"

"It's the gun in my back belt. It's starting to come out. Can you grab it?"

"I can try," Williston said, edging closer. In the dim starlight he could make out Lansing's general form. He guessd at the approximate position of the gun. He raked his hand blindly, his fingertips brushing the handle of the gun, knocking it from Lansing's belt.

"Oh, shit!" Williston swore softly.

The gun clattered briefly against the wall of the canyon befor hitting the rocks below them and discharging.

"What was that?" Hatch yelled from the canyon floor behind them.

"They got down!" Reid shouted. "They're shooting at us!"

Reid started blasting away with his M-16 on automatic. The only light in the canyon was the muzzle flashes of the assault rifle.

"Reid! Hatch! What the hell are you shooting at?" The voice came from a third man.

"Who was that?" Lansing asked in a loud whisper.

"I don't know," Williston admitted, "but now's not the time to ask. Let's get out of here."

Lansing sidestepped along the ledge as quickly as he dared. He could hear Williston right behind him. It was just a few minutes before the sheriff could discern the dark shape of a piñon tree. The tree grew on the canyon side of the ledge. Lansing knew they had almost reached safety.

In the canyon below the three men were now talking in hushed tones. When Williston and Lansing reached the cover of the small tree, they looked down at the canyon floor. Two flashlights were scanning the rocks and trees along the base of the wall. The beams were strong enough that had the two men still been on the rock face, they could have been seen.

"Let's make tracks," Lansing said. "There's got to be another way out of this canyon."

"Just don't go too fast," Williston pleaded. "Between riding a horse all morning and getting the crap kicked out of me, I'm starting to stiffen up."

"Just keep in mind how stiff you'll be if those guys get hold of you, Senator."

"Point well taken. Let's go."

The path they were following began a descent to the canyon floor. They followed it for a half mile before it disappeared altogether. Part had crumbled into the valley floor. The rest was covered by a rock slide. The slope was gentle enough that the two men could scramble the final thirty feet to the bottom with no problem.

The flashlights were no longer coming toward them, looking instead in the direction of the cliff dwelling.

"What do you think's going on?" Williston asked.

"They may have found my gun, which means they'll know we're unarmed. They won't waste any time getting up to those buildings. It may take them an hour to figure out we're not there. That may be just long enough for us to get the hell out of here."

"Yeah," Williston sounded pessimistic, "if there is a way out."

Lansing started for the far end of the canyon. Their progress was slow. There was no defined path and the occasional streambed was covered with loose rocks. In the dim light it was hard to tell if the steep canyon walls afforded any practical way out. Thirty minutes later they still hadn't reached the end of the canyon. They were both tired.

Lansing sat on a small boulder and surveyed the

canyon rim. The top portion of the western rim was being lit by the rising moon. In a couple of hours the entire canyon would be awash in moonlight. The sheriff did not want to be caught in the open when that happened.

Rubble from eons of erosion sloped against the sandstone cliffs. The walls above the rubble extended still another hundred feet to the rim.

"What now?" Williston asked from his own boulder a few feet away.

"We don't have much choice," Lansing said grimly. "As soon as the guys down there"—he pointed down the canyon—"figure out *we're* not down there, they're going to be up here. Besides, if your Indian friend found a way out of here, we sure as hell can."

"I'm not so sure he climbed out," Williston said doubtfully. "I'm starting to believe there's a reason for him to be called Windwalker."

"I guess they'll have to call me Rockcrawler, 'cause that's the only way I figure we'll get out."

Lansing began climbing the slippery slope of debris. Williston sat on his boulder and watched as his companion searched for a starting point. The senator didn't realize how tired he was. He didn't even know he'd dozed off until Lansing shook him awake.

"Senator, you all right?" the sheriff asked.

"Yeah, sure," Williston responded wearily.

"I think I found a way up. You game?"

Williston was surprised at how bright the canyon was becoming from the moonlight. "I think so, as long as it doesn't entail any physical effort."

"I'm making no guarantees on that," Lansing said, helping the senator to his feet. "It's at the very end of the canyon. It looks like there used to be a way out of here at one time. Part of the cliff face fell in, blocking off the exit. It's steep, but I think we can make it."

"Lead on," Williston said. "But I'm going to let you know right now, you're hearing from my travel agent when I get home. I don't recommend this vacation for anyone."

# 30

**Bets was confident she could handle Lansing's horse.** For the first ten minutes, everything went smoothly. But when they reached a point along the canyon rim where they could cut toward the west, the horse refused.

Bets tugged on the reins, telling the horse she wanted to turn left. The horse simply tugged in the opposite direction and continued straight ahead.

"What's wrong?" Carerra asked.

"For some reason he doesn't want to go that way." She gestured toward the access to the open desert.

"Maybe he's afraid?"

"Yeah," Elizabeth agreed, "and maybe he's stubborn."

The rider tried a different ploy. She pulled the reins to the right, trying to make the horse turn around in the opposite direction. The horse stubbornly pulled his head to the left and kept walking in the northerly direction they had been following.

The girl reined the horse to a stop. Dismounting, Elizabeth held the bridle in her hand. "Come on, boy. We want to go this way." She pulled the reins and started walking toward the path leading away from the canyon. The horse jerked back on the leather strap, refusing to budge.

"What's wrong with this animal?" Bets complained.

"He doesn't want to go where you want to go," Carerra observed. "Maybe there's someplace he wants to take us."

"Where?"

"Maybe he knows where Sheriff Lansing is. Maybe he's trying to take us there."

"I guess we go with him or we walk."

"So far I find riding a hell of a lot more comfortable," Carerra commented. "Besides, could be Lansing needs our help."

"Okay, Doctor," Elizabeth said, climbing back into the saddle. "I'm with the two of you."

Lansing's horse continued on his course, following the rim of the canyon. Both women kept a lookout for anything unusual along the trail that would indicate someone had been there earlier.

After nearly twenty minutes, Elizabeth finally asked, "How much farther are we going, horse?"

As if in direct response to the question, the horse left the ridge and began a descent into the canyon. In the growing moonlight, both women could tell the path into the canyon was well defined. Even so, the moon was not high enough to illuminate the entire ravine. The path disappeared into complete darkness.

"I hope he knows what he's doing," Carerra complained. "I can't see a damned thing down there."

"He sure acts like he's been here before." Bets tried to sound reassuring.

"I think I'd feel more secure if I knew how far I'd fall before hitting bottom," the doctor commented, tightening her grip on Elizabeth.

Bets had the typical self-confidence of a teenager who knows she's too young to die. "Just don't look down."

"I don't know why not. There's nothing to see."

As their descent took them below the angle of the moon's rays, their eyes adjusted to the darkness of the chasm. The canyon floor seemed deceptively close. Its actual distance became apparent when it took ten minutes to reach the bottom.

The horse didn't waver from his course. On the canyon floor he proceeded ahead, not changing his pace. Elizabeth and Carerra continued looking for something out of the ordinary, some sign someone else had been there recently.

Had the light in the canyon been brighter, they would have seen the numerous hoof tracks on the sandy streambed. It wasn't until they came upon the carcass of a dead pony that they were assured they were following a recent trail.

Lansing's horse stopped and sniffed the air. Elizabeth dismounted to check the dead pony. "She was shot," Bets said in no more than a whisper. She noticed the different tracks in the sand. "It looks like a lot of people have been through here recently." She looked up at Carerra. "Should we keep going?"

"Why don't you get back on the horse and see what he wants to do," the doctor suggested.

Elizabeth got back in the saddle. "Okay, boy. Do your stuff."

The horse continued up the canyon. They followed the twisting streambed for another quarter of a mile when they came upon three saddled horses. The two women dismounted and approached the knot of animals. The reins had been tied to low bushes.

"Well, they didn't just wander here," Bets whispered, indicating the reins. "But where are their owners?"

Carerra was wondering that herself. She began looking around for any sign of another human. A few feet away she found the end of a rope lying on the ground. Picking it up, she discovered it stretched up the embankment. She gave the rope a tug. It was securely fastened to the rocks somewhere above them.

"Elizabeth, look at this."

The young woman joined her friend. "Where do you think it goes?"

"It doesn't look like it goes anywhere," Carerra commented.

"There's one way to find out." Elizabeth started following the rope.

"Where are you going?" Carerra demanded.

"To see where this rope leads. Somebody put it here for a reason."

"Elizabeth, I really don't feel like playing Nancy Drew right now."

"You said Sheriff Lansing may be in trouble. His horse brought us here. Maybe this rope will lead us to him."

"Damn. I hate it when someone uses my own words to force me to do something. Especially if it's something I don't want to do. All right, let's follow the rope."

They traced the rope along the bottom of a wash. As they climbed the embankment they still had no guess as to where it would lead.

The end of the rope, they discovered, was secured around a small outcropping of rocks. There was nothing else around the rope.

"Okay. Now what?" Carerra asked.

Elizabeth looked at the rock wall another twenty feet above them. "Maybe we haven't gone far enough," she suggested.

"Elizabeth, I don't see anything up there."

Bets ignored the remark and continued her climb.

Carerra stood and watched. Her legs were beginning to ache. She was tired. All she wanted to do was lie down and go to sleep.

"Margarite, come here!" Bets whispered as loudly as she could.

Carerra sighed wearily and began the final ascent. When she reached the top of the wash, Bets had disappeared.

"Elizabeth? Where are you?"

Bets popped out from a slit in the rock. "It's a cave. They must have gone in here."

"Well, we're not going in there. I'm drawing the line right now."

"Come on, Margarite. We have to find out."

"Listen, young lady. We don't know what's in there. There could be a hundred-foot drop. We could get ourselves killed."

"You're right." Elizabeth pushed past Carerra and started down the hill. "Wait here."

"Where are you going?"

"I'm going to see if there's a flashlight in one of the saddle bags. I'll be right back."

Carerra sat down. It was becoming obvious to her that when Elizabeth made up her mind to do something, nothing would stop her. The McGaffrey girl returned a few minutes later. She had a flashlight in one hand and the rope from the rock slung over her shoulder.

"I'm going to tie one end around me," she said as she uncoiled the rope. "You hang on to the other end. If I slip or something, you can keep me from falling."

"We have one more option. We can wait and see if anyone comes out."

"They can't if they're hurt," Bets observed, tying a double knot in the rope. She switched on the flashlight. "Ready?"

Carerra picked up the remainder of the rope. "No, I'm not."

Bets pointed the flashlight into the darkness and

stepped inside the tunnel. "Looks like there's a bend up ahead about ten feet."

Carerra stood in the entrance feeding her partner rope.

As Elizabeth rounded the bend in the tunnel, she shone the light at the far end. "I think it's safe to come in, Margarite. There's another bend in the cave up ahead."

Dr. Carerra tentatively entered the passage, bringing the rope with her. Elizabeth waited for the doctor to reach her before continuing. Carerra then let the younger woman get twenty feet ahead of her before following again.

Elizabeth stopped at the next corner and waited for Carerra to catch up. Bets shone the light down the passageway. There was yet another bend in the rock wall, this one only twenty or so feet away. Carerra waited at the corner as Bets made her way to the next bend.

"It's a way out!" Bets exclaimed. "And there's a campfire out there."

Carerra hurried down the passage. Elizabeth had already stepped into the open. They had emerged into a second canyon. Fifty feet away, near the bottom of the canyon wall, was a small fire. There was no one around the fire.

The two women approached the light.

"They must be around here somewhere!" Elizabeth whispered.

"Down on your faces! Now!" A man's voice barked from behind them. There was the unmistakable click-click of a rifle cartridge being chambered. "And I have a gun on you, so don't do anything stupid."

## 31

"Do as he says," Carerra ordered, sinking to her knees, then stretching out on the ground. Elizabeth did as she was instructed. "Listen, mister," the doctor began, "I don't know what's going on here. I don't want to know. We've been lost in these canyons since before dark. We were just trying to find a way out."

"Shut up!" Reid ordered. "You think I'm stupid or somethin'? You didn't find that tunnel by accident. You were lookin' for somethin'."

"Honest," Bets pleaded. "It's like Dr. Carerra said. We were lost and found your horses in the other canyon. Your rope led us to the tunnel. . . . We just wanted someone to help us out of here."

"Yeah, right," the gunman snorted. "Why don't you just shut up like I told ya?"

"Can we at least sit up?" Margarite asked.

"No," came the flat response.

Carerra turned her head to look at Elizabeth. The girl was just a few feet away. Her eyes were open. The look on her face reflected more anger than fear. "You okay?" the doctor whispered.

"Yeah," Elizabeth whispered in return.

"Just do what this S.O.B. tells us to do for now. There has to be someone else around." Carerra felt a sudden, swift pain in the bottom of her foot where Reid kicked her.

"I told ya! Shut up!"

"Listen, you . . ." Carerra said angrily, starting to get up.

Reid stomped her with the bottom of his boot, this time in the middle of her back. Carerra sprawled face first in the dirt. "You damn women are all alike! Nothing ever sinks in till ya get slapped around. . . . I told ya! Shut up and lay still."

Carerra understood the ground rules now. As angry as she was, there was nothing she could do at that moment. She knew she was dealing with a man who did not understand reason. He'd just as soon beat on her as look at her. She knew the type too well. There had been three other horses in the other canyon. There were probably two other people nearby. She'd bide her time until someone else arrived.

She tried to make herself as comfortable as possible. To quell her anger she concentrated on the heat from the fire a few feet away. The night was turning cool and the little warmth she was getting was welcome. In a few minutes she was asleep.

Carerra didn't realize where she was or why she was there when she heard the shout: "Reid, you still down there?"

"Yeah!"

The second shout came from a man standing next to the doctor. The bellow shook her into consciousness. She could still feel the warmth of the fire. A few feet away Elizabeth McGaffrey lay on the ground, her head resting on her folded arms. Her eyes were closed.

The doctor couldn't tell if she'd been asleep a minute or an hour. She felt rested and was acutely aware of the sounds around her.

"We didn't find anything. We're coming down."

The voice seemed to come from the canyon wall above them. She wondered how long it would take the new arrivals to reach the bottom: fifteen, twenty minutes? She hoped she and Elizabeth would be dealing with more civilized men.

"Well, be polite when you get here," Reid called back. "We have company."

"What do you mean?" asked the man above them.

"You'll see when you get here," Reid said with a laugh.

The doctor looked at her companion. Elizabeth's eyes were open. She, too, was listening to everything that was going on. It was less than five minutes before the two men arrived.

"Who are they?" Hatch asked.

"They came wanderin' through the tunnel over there about a half hour ago. . . . You didn't find those two bastards up there?"

*They're looking for two men,* Carerra thought. She hoped one of them was Lansing.

"No." Hatch walked over and tapped the muzzle of his rifle on Carerra's shoulder. "You two. Get up. Let's have a look at you."

Carerra pushed herself off the ground, brushing the dirt and sand from her as she stood. Elizabeth did the same. Carerra didn't recognize any of the three men.

"Well, well, well," said the third man. "Look who's here."

"What d'ya mean?" Reid asked.

The third man stepped into the light of the fire. Carerra heard a gasp from Elizabeth. "You don't recognize the young lady, Reid?" Reid shook his head no. "This is little Betsy McGaffrey."

"Mack McGaffrey's kid?" Hatch asked. "What's she doing here?"

"Who the hell knows? She thinks she's an independent little princess who doesn't have to answer to anyone." The man stepped forward and squeezed her cheeks. "Isn't that right, princess?"

Elizabeth slapped the man's hand away. "Leave me alone, Parker!"

"Oh, we're going to be feisty, huh?" He slapped her hard enough to knock her to the ground.

Carerra immediately jumped at Parker. "You leave her alone!"

Reid had been keeping an eye on the doctor. He grabbed her and threw her on the ground next to Elizabeth. "You just don't listen, do ya?" Reid spat.

"Who's your friend?" Parker asked, addressing Bets.

"I'm Dr. Margarite Carerra. What's it to you?"

"It's plenty to me. I want to know why you're here."

"We got lost!" Elizabeth snapped. "We told that to your baboon over there."

"Now, now," Parker corrected in feigned politeness. "Let's not go calling people names. Remember? I told you you'd wish you'd made some friends around that ranch. Right now it looks like you could use all the friends you can get." He turned to Reid. "Go check on the horses. Make sure there's no one else out there."

"All right." He left, sounding disappointed he wouldn't be there for the interrogation.

"Hatch. Cut up that rope around the girl's waist and tie them up." Parker held the gun on them while Hatch worked.

"I demand that you let us go!" Carerra insisted.

"Ma'am, I don't think you're in a position to make demands," Parker observed. "Now, let's try it again. What are you doing here?"

"Elizabeth told you," Carerra explained. "We were lost."

"What were you doing on the Anasazi Strip to begin with?"

"We were out for a drive in my Jeep," Elizabeth interrupted. "The Jeep broke down and we had to walk. There's no law against that."

"No, but you didn't drive here. There aren't any roads this far back in the hills. What were you doing?"

"Nothing," Elizabeth insisted.

"Somebody send you?"

"No, of course not." Elizabeth winced when Hatch started tying her hands behind her back. "Why are you doing this?"

"I don't want you to wander off and get hurt in the dark."

"Just wait till my father finds out about this."

"Right now I don't care what your father finds out." He knelt close to the girl. "But I will tell you a little secret, Sweet Betsy. I don't think your father would care. You're a spoiled brat who's been nothing but a pain in the ass. If anything happened to you I think your father would be grateful."

"You're a bastard," Carerra remarked.

"That's the nicest thing a pretty woman has said to me all day," Parker sneered. "'Is there anything you want to add?"

"I have nothing to say to you at all," the doctor said, turning her head away.

Parker stood. "We'll see."

Hatch first tied their hands behind their backs, then trussed their feet. He had both women securely bound by the time Reid got back from checking the horses.

"There's another horse out there," Reid reported.

"Another horse?" Parker turned to Bets. "I thought your story was you had walked."

"We did walk, till we found the horse. Then we rode."

"Where'd you find the horse?"

"Up on the canyon rim, a couple of miles south of here," Bets explained.

"Bet ya it's the sheriff's horse," Reid inserted.

"Shut up!" Hatch barked. "Don't you ever know when to keep quiet!"

Carerra looked at Reid. "What happened to the sheriff?"

"Nothin'. Nothin' happened to the sheriff." Reid responded defensively.

"Reid, you got a big mouth," Parker said in disgust. He turned back to Elizabeth. "I'm not playing games, Sweet Betsy. I want to know what you two are doing up here. I want to know who knows you're here. And I'll remind you, there's no one around who can help you."

"I told you the truth. We got lost."

"I don't believe her, Parker," Reid said.

"Why don't you shut up," Parker snorted. "All right, Sweet Betsy. You just sit here and think about it. I also want you to think about what I could do to you if I don't like your answer." He picked up a flashlight and tossed it to Reid. "Hatch, watch these two. Reid and I are going to take a stroll down the canyon."

"What for?" Reid asked warily.

"I'll explain it to you. But if it makes you feel any better, bring your rifle."

The two men set off into the moonlit canyon.

Hatch threw a few scraps of wood onto the fire. Picking up a smaller twig, he held it in the fire until it started to burn. He used the flame from the twig to light a cigarette.

"Why are you keeping us here?" Carerra asked. "We haven't done anything."

Hatch ignored her. Picking up his rifle, he walked a few feet away and sat down, his back against a rock. With the rifle lying across his lap, he finished his cigarette, then tipped his hat to cover his eyes. In a few minutes he was snoring.

"What do you think they're going to do to us?" Elizabeth whispered.

"I don't know," Carerra admitted. "I hope they'll realize we don't know anything and let us go."

"What about the sheriff? If something's happened to him, they know we'll blame them."

"You heard them talking. They're looking for two men. If we're lucky, one of them is Sheriff Lansing, which means he's around here somewhere."

"I hope the other one is Senator Williston."

"Me, too, Elizabeth. Me too."

# 32

WILLISTON DIDN'T REALIZE HOW TIRED HE WAS UNTIL HE started following Lansing. His legs were stiff and sore. He ached from the bruises he'd earned from the encounter with Reid. His arms were heavy from the climbing he had done throughout the day.

"You know what, Sheriff? I always prided myself on how good a shape I was in for a man in his mid-fifties," Williston remarked, trying to keep pace with Lansing.

"I don't think you're doing bad at all," Lansing commented, trying not to let his own weariness show. "For an old man."

"That's not even a joke, right now. I feel like an old man." He found it harder to breathe with every step.

"It's probably the altitude," the sheriff said, noticing his companion's labored breathing. "We're over six thousand feet in this part of the state. You're just not used to the thin air. Keep reminding yourself it's the elevation that's getting to you, not your physical condition."

"I'll do that," the senator wheezed.

They reached the sloping rubble that Lansing hoped would lead to an escape route. From where they stood, the rim of the canyon appeared to be lower than the surrounding cliffs. The barrier looked broken and boulder strewn, as if the walls had collapsed from opposite sides of the canyon.

The sheriff started climbing the incline. Instead of going straight up, he attacked the steep bank at a slant. His intent was to zigzag his way to the bottom of the broken cliff face. From there it would be a matter of finding enough footholds and handholds to negotiate the final sixty or seventy feet.

Williston let the sheriff get several feet ahead before following. The vertical progress was slow. They had to travel a slanting distance of nearly fifty feet for every ten feet in elevation. Even with that shallow an attack on the embankment, they found themselves occasionally losing ground.

After what seemed an hour, Williston looked up at the canyon wall they still needed to climb. It seemed farther away than ever. He told himself he had to rest. He forced himself to reach the side of the canyon where he had a solid rock cliff to lean against. The canyon floor was thirty feet below him. There was still another thirty feet of embankment to negotiate.

Williston sat with his right side leaning against the canyon wall. The grade was too steep to sit with his back against the rock. He closed his eyes for just a moment. As he dozed, he felt the embankment start to give way beneath him. He opened his eyes with a start, expecting to find himself sliding toward the canyon floor below.

Instead, he discovered he was falling backward. The dirt, gravel, and stones of the slope, along with him, were sliding into a hole in the cliff wall, buried eons earlier by the avalanche that had blocked the canyon.

Williston managed to yell, "Lansing!" before he was swallowed by the earth. Lansing turned just in time to see Williston disappear.

"Oh, my God!" Lansing swore, scrambling across the slope to the spot where Williston had just been. At the base of the rock wall was an opening three feet in diameter. Dust was still billowing from the hole. Lansing tried to fan the dust from the air. "Senator," he shouted into the hole. "Are you all right?"

There was no response.

"Senator Williston, can you hear me?"

Lansing could hear the echo of his voice, but nothing else. The echo told him the cave below him was big and probably deep. That didn't make him feel any better. It was dark and he wasn't about to crawl inside without some kind of light. Whenever he was in the back country, he always carried essentials in his saddle bag in case of emergencies. Unfortunately, he thought, his saddle bag, along with his horse, had nearly reached Las Palmas by now.

He slid down the embankment to the canyon floor. Because water had ceased flowing through the canyon hundreds of years earlier, scrub brush and other vegetation had taken hold along the canyon floor. Even in the dim light of the moon he managed to find what he needed. Several creosote bushes had rooted in the rocky soil of the gorge. He tore a dozen branches from the largest of the evergreen bushes.

Going back to the embankment, he gathered several handfuls of dried grass and made a small pile. He pulled two bullets from his cartridge belt. Using the small hunting knife he always carried, he pulled the leadslugs from the shells and carefully dumped the black powder into a pile beneath the grass.

Lansing knew most of the rocks in this part of the country were sandstone. But other types of rock could always be found in the streambeds, even of old, long-dried streams. Looking on the ground next to him, he found two dark stones, rounded ages earlier by forgotten floods.

Cracking the rocks together, he broke one in half. The sharp edge gave him a striking surface. With the dull side of his knife he began hammering the steel against the stone. It took five strikes before he produced his first spark.

The spark died before it reached the black powder.

He held the stone and knife closer to the kindling and began striking the implements together again. The second spark missed its target. The third spark hit the black powder, causing it to produce a bright flash. The flash of the powder was intense enough to kindle a few strands of grass.

Lansing dropped the rock and began nursing the fire. In less than a minute all the grass in the pile was blazing. The sheriff placed more grass and small twigs on the fire to make it hotter. He looked down the canyon to see if there were any approaching lights. The canyon still appeared empty.

He built the fire a little stronger. When he was sure the fire could sustain itself without his care, he held the leafy end of a creosote branch over the fire. The branch started to crackle and sputter as the resin caught fire. The odor of the burning branch was strong. Lansing was grateful there was no breeze to carry the aroma down the canyon.

Once he was sure the branch was safely lit, he kicked dirt over his small grass fire to put it out. Stomping out the tiny embers, he kicked the blackened ashes apart to hide the fact that there had been a fire. Sheathing his knife, he picked up the rest of his impromptu torches and scrambled up the embankment to Williston's cave.

"Senator, can you hear me? It's Cliff Lansing," the sheriff called into the opening. There was still no response. The flame on his makeshift torch had dwindled to embers. He blew on the glowing leaves and in a moment he had light again.

Lansing stuck the torch into the opening. The meager light of the torch was swallowed by the darkness. He could see nothing.

"Damn, I hate caves," Lansing said to himself.

Making sure he had a firm hold on his unused torches, he started crawling backward into the opening. Before he was halfway through the entrance he found himself sliding helplessly into the cave with no way of stopping. He forgot about his creosote branches as he desperately tried to grasp anything that would slow his plunge. There was nothing within reach.

When he finally hit the cave floor, his one lit torch lay a few feet away, nearly extinguished. He grabbed the branch and frantically blew the flame back to life as he choked on the suffocating dust.

As the dust settled and the torch began to blaze again, he realized there was no sign of Senator Williston.

# 33

"SENATOR WILLISTON?" LANSING CALLED, TRYING TO FAN THE dust from his face. "It's Cliff Lansing! Do you hear me?"

The only response was Lansing's own voice reverberating through the cavern.

Lansing gathered the creosote branches and picked up his hat. Using the dwindling flame of his first torch, he lit a second branch. It took a moment before the green leaves ignited. Inside the cave he found the pungent odor of the burning resin almost overpowering. He tried to keep the flame away from his head as much as possible.

With the new flame he was able to survey his surroundings. The small entrance he used to enter the cave was twelve to fifteen feet above his head, level with the ceiling. The original entrance had been thirty feet wide before it was blocked by a large slab of sandstone and other debris from a rock slide. From where he stood, it didn't appear he could go out the same way he entered, at least not without a ladder.

He looked around on the floor for any sign of Williston. There was nothing to indicate the senator had been there. Lansing turned and looked down the corridor.

"I guess we go this way," the sheriff said out loud. He suddenly realized he found the sound of his own voice reassuring. "It's almost as if you're not by yourself," he observed.

Holding the torch above his head, he began moving deeper into the cave. After thirty feet the cave began to get larger as the floor gradually sloped downward. Fifty feet from the entrance the cave suddenly expanded into a huge cavern. The size was breathtaking. The floor dropped rapidly away and the ceiling was now thirty feet above his head.

For a sense of security Lansing moved closer to the cavern wall. He felt too exposed in the vast chamber. It was when he moved next to the wall that he noticed the petroglyphs. Hundreds of drawings had been carved into the rock. Many of the drawings were arcane symbols he had seen in museum displays of Native American art. Others depicted animals and humans. There were some images he could not identify. Most of the icons were embellished by yellow, red, and turquoise pigments, still rich and brilliant.

Distracted by the artwork, Lansing failed to notice the sudden drop in the floor. Nearly falling, he jumped back a few feet. He thought for a moment he had almost stepped over a ledge. Holding the light closer to the ground, he discovered he was standing at the top of a wide stairway. The steps had been roughly cut into the native rock. Following the contour of the cavern wall, the steps descended deeper into the mountain.

There had been no sign of Williston and no other passages to follow.

"Looks like we keep going this way," he muttered.

Lansing tested the first step. He put half his weight, then his full weight, on the stone. It felt solid. Satisfied he would not fall through, he tested the next few in the same manner. Confident the floor was not going to crumble beneath him, he continued down the steps.

The petroglyphs continued to embellish the walls. But as Lansing descended into the cave the pictures became more stylized and the creatures more bizarre and less identifiable. He stepped back a few feet to get a better perspective.

The symbols were not randomly placed pictures, thrown on the wall wherever there was space. He was looking at a mural that told a story. The farther he went down the steps, the older the story. The creatures he couldn't identify at first suddenly became recognizable and they were part of the story.

In one scene was a cave bear, four times the size of the men fighting it. In another scene the bodies of men, women, and children were being ravaged by a saber-toothed tiger. In yet another picture a group of hunters surrounded a woolly mammoth caught in a bog.

Lansing's fascination was so intense, he hadn't realized he had reached the bottom of the steps. He lit another creosote branch. Holding the torch above his head, he could see he had descended forty feet below the entry level. Giant stalactites and stalagmites decorated the cavern. Some were so ancient they had joined to form columns.

From somewhere even deeper in the cavern came the plinking sound of water dripping.

Lansing wasn't sure what effect a loud noise would have in these ancient caverns. He called softly into the darkness, "Senator Williston?"

The only response was the continual dripping of water.

Lansing followed the sound. The larger cavern led to a smaller passageway, similar in size to the entry tunnel. Jars, pitchers, and other pottery pieces sat in niches carved into the walls. Rows of spears, atlatls, war clubs, and bows and arrows lined the walls. The weapons were arranged so that a man could run past the armory, grab his equipment, and head for the defense of the cavern. The sheriff guessed the pottery along the walls once contained provisions to sustain the defenders.

Smaller passageways intersected the corridor Lansing followed. He hoped by staying in the main passage he could find his way back. Lansing's innate fear of caves was overcome by the wonders held in the catacombs he was following. He was also intensely curious about where Williston could have gone.

As the flame began to die on his torch he noticed a dim glow in the distance. He quickly lit another branch and hurried toward the light.

The main corridor bent gradually toward the right. As it curved around it expanded into a second cavern, though not as large as the first. On a stone pallet at the far end of the chamber was Williston. His arms were folded across his chest.

The room was lit by dozens of small pottery lamps, the flames fed by tallow and beeswax.

An old man with long white hair sat in front of the pallet. His back was to Lansing. As he got closer, Lansing could hear the old man chanting softly. Williston did not move. There was a deep gash on the senator's forehead that had stopped bleeding. There was no color to his face.

Lansing tried to say something, but his mouth and throat felt painfully dry. The words wouldn't come.

Suddenly, from behind Lansing, came the wailing sound of wind rushing through the caverns. The sheriff turned in time to see a wall of dust and sand surge toward him. He instinctively dove to the floor and covered his face with his arms. He felt the grains of sand pelt his exposed skin and the wind rip at his clothing as his hat was torn away. The howl of the wind was almost deafening. Lansing couldn't imagine where the wind came from or how long it would last.

Then it stopped, as quickly as it started.

Lansing ventured a peek. The room was still. He reached for his torch but the fire was extinguished. He sat up and turned toward the stone pallet. The small pottery lamps were still lit, despite the passing maelstrom. The chanter was now kneeling next to Williston, helping him sit up.

The sheriff hurried to the two men. "Senator, are you all right?"

"What?" Williston gingerly touched his forehead. "Yes. I think so." He noticed the old man next to him. "Windwalker! You're alive."

"And so are you," the Watcher said. He reached next to the pallet and picked up a small bowl. "Drink this."

Williston was still groggy and had to use both hands to drink from the bowl. He grimaced at the taste. "This is awful."

"I know," Windwalker admitted. "It will make you stronger."

Williston finished the contents. He looked at Lansing, then back to Windwalker. "What happened?"

"You fell," Lansing explained. "Into a cave. What do you remember?"

"I remember . . . I remember we were climbing up to that cliff. And I sat down to rest. . . . I fell asleep. I had the strangest dream that I was falling. . . ." He looked at Lansing. "You said I fell into a cave?"

The sheriff nodded.

"I remember everything going black. . . ." He looked at Windwalker. "Then the *a'doshle* came. The ones that were in the kiva. They took me by the arms and we flew through the darkness. It seemed like we were flying up. And above us was a light. A round light . . . like at the end of a tunnel.

"All of a sudden we flew out of this shaft and were

in the sky. The stars were out . . . the moon. I could look down and see the ground below me. Then the *a'doshle* told me I had to go back."

"They spoke to you?" Windwalker asked.

"In a way. I didn't understand the words but I knew what they meant. Does that make sense?"

The old man nodded.

Williston noticed the sheriff. "Lansing, you're looking at me as if I'm nuts."

"No, sir." Lansing shook his head. "I've seen some strange things tonight. I think I'd believe just about anything right now."

The senator looked back at Windwalker. "They told me I had to come back because I wasn't finished. Then they told me . . ." He concentrated for a moment. "They told me I had to return the *Shipap* to the Human Beings . . . that the time had come. After that I woke up and I was here. . . . Do you know what any of this means?"

Windwalker fixed his stare on a small flame. "In the fourteenth year of the fourteenth cycle a man will find his soul. He will do battle with the Destroyer. And when he is victorious he will return the *Shipap* to the Human Beings."

"You're not talking about me," Williston said.

"You had the vision, Senator Williston. You were told you had to return the *Shipap* to the Humans."

"How can I?" Williston complained. "I don't even know where it is."

Windwalker spread his arms apart, palms up. "As you sit here now, Senator Williston, you are in the *Shipap*."

# 34

"YOU MEAN THIS . . . CAVE . . . IS THE *SHIPAP*?"

Windwalker nodded.

"I don't know what the *Shipap* is supposed to be, Senator," Lansing commented, "but there's a lot more to this place than just this room. It could go on for miles. There are cave drawings that must date back ten thousand years . . . back to the Ice Age."

"Cave drawings?" Williston sounded surprised.

"There are pictures of mastodons and saber-toothed tigers and . . . cavemen, I guess is what you'd call them. There's pottery. There's a whole arsenal of weapons. . . . I don't think anyone's been around for quite a while, but there's a lot of stuff they left behind."

"Then this is the *Shipap*!" Williston smiled at Windwalker. "Your legends make sense. The Human Beings lived in here, in the dark, while the winter raged outside during the last Ice Age. Then the Great Spirit melted away the snows and brought light to the outside . . . and the Anasazi emerged from the hole in the ground to the new world."

Williston stood and looked around him with new realization. "My God, this is the greatest archeological discovery in the New World this century! Maybe of all time!"

Windwalker looked at Williston doubtfully. "It must be given back to the Human Beings. The *a'doshle* told you."

"Don't you realize, Windwalker, a place like this has to belong to all mankind. Not just a few. Not just the Zuni nation."

"It belongs to the Human Beings. It is their heritage. It is their chance for survival. The disease that visited their reservation last year will be the first of many. Unless they return to their rightful land and practice their ancient beliefs they will die.

"This is why you were brought here. So you would understand. So you would know the stories are true.

"You have seen the *a'doshle.* They have spoken to you. You must do as they have asked."

"Some of the stories are true," Williston said, sitting on the pallet in front of the Watcher. "I'll grant you that. They make sense. There's a rational explanation for the beliefs.

"But the world out there is a real world, made out of solid objects that can be touched or smelled or tasted. There are physical explanations for every phenomenon we experience.

"The *Shipap* is real. I know that now. But I fell. I had a dream. I dreamt about the things you and I talked about. That does not make my dream real."

"Was that a dream in the kiva?" the Indian asked.

"That was a . . . a hallucination. Somehow you were able to hypnotize me into thinking I saw something."

"Was it real when the *a'doshle* stared into your soul and you trembled?"

Williston stopped and thought about the experience in the kiva. The lights in the pottery lamps danced and flickered at the question. The shadows on the cave walls took on individual personalities. To the senator, the silhouettes demanded an answer. He suddenly felt very cold and lonely.

He didn't want to answer the Watcher's question. Instead, he asked one of his own. "Who is the Destroyer?"

"Only you know that," Windwalker replied.

"How am I supposed to help you if you won't help me?" Williston asked angrily.

"I cannot give an answer I do not know. And if you do not know, it will be revealed to you. But you have had the vision. You are the conduit for the *a'doshle.*"

Williston turned from the old Zuni and stared into the darkness of the caverns. His fifty-five-year-old pragmatic belief system was being overwhelmed by emotions stirred by a pagan spiritualism. It didn't make any sense to him. There was always an explanation for hearing something going bump in the night. There were no spooks. There was no bogeyman. How could he let a shriveled old white-haired fool convince him otherwise? He held his hands together to keep them from trembling.

"Senator, I wish I knew what you two were talking about," Lansing interrupted. "Maybe I could help. But right now we have a more immediate problem."

"What?" Williston asked absently.

"There are still a few guys out in that canyon who want to see all three of us dead. Unless we find a way out of here, there's a good chance that could happen."

The senator pushed aside his self-doubts. "Yeah, you're right." He turned to the old man. "Is there a way out of here, besides the hole I fell through?"

"Yes. There is a passage that leads to the canyon rim."

"Can you take us there?" Lansing asked.

"Yes." Windwalker stood.

Lansing looked around the cave. "We need to get out of here before they find the entrance we used."

"The *a'doshle* will not let them enter the *Shipap,*" the old man assured him.

"Even so . . ." Lansing observed, "getting out of here is only half our worry. We still need to hoof it to town without getting caught in the open."

"Before we leave, you should know that the three men in the canyon have captured two white women."

"Women?" the sheriff asked. "Who?"

"I do not know them," the Watcher admitted. "They are at the far end of the canyon, near the dwellings."

"Can you show us where they are?" Lansing pressed.

"I will show you from the canyon rim." Windwalker picked up a small pottery lamp. "Follow me."

The exit from the *Shipap* was not far from the ceremonial room where Lansing had found the other two men. They had to follow a short maze of passages until they reached a tunnel with a slight incline. The tunnel became increasingly steeper until it bent into a vertical shaft.

Williston looked up the chimney. "The story of the kiva." He looked at Windwalker. "This was what the Human Beings were taught to remember. This place right here."

"This was part of it," Windwalker admitted, "but not all."

Handholds and toeholds had been cut into the rock walls. There was no light coming from the upper reaches of the shaft, so it was impossible to judge how far they had to climb.

Windwalker set his lamp down and began the climb. Williston went up next, then Lansing. The sheriff found the climbing slow. The two white men, at least, had to grope their way from one hold to the next. Lansing overtook the senator several times before they finally reached the top.

When they emerged onto the surface, they found a large boulder overhanging the opening. Several other boulders of similar size populated the surrounding field.

"I'm not sure I could have found that opening even if you told me where it was," Lansing commented, looking back at the large rocks.

"It is a long-forgotten place." Windwalker nodded, leading them back to the canyon. "It was not supposed to be found."

The trek back to the canyon rim was over a mile from the entrance to the *Shipap*. Their way was well lit, though the moon was past its zenith and on the western side of its journey.

When they reached the edge of the canyon, Lansing shook his head. "I've spent a lifetime in this country and I'll be damned if I can tell one canyon from the next."

"This is the one," Windwalker said. "The cliff dwelling is farther down. They have built a fire on the canyon floor. We will see them easily."

Another half hour passed before they reached their destination. Windwalker stooped as he approached the canyon rim. The last few feet he lay on his stomach and crawled to the edge. Lansing and Williston imitated their guide, eventually flanking him as they looked into the canyon.

At first Lansing wasn't convinced they were at the right spot. He expected to see the cliff dwellings looming on the opposite wall of the canyon from where they were. The light of the moon had moved, so the far canyon wall was shrouded in shadows. He understood why the small city had gone undetected for centuries.

Below them on the canyon floor, just as Windwalker had predicted, was a small campfire. A few feet away from the fire were two people, both with long hair, both with their hands tied behind their backs. Another person sat separately from the others, his back against a rock. It looked like he had a rifle laid across his lap.

One of the women, the one with black hair, turned her head so that her face was exposed to the men on the rim. The woman was almost two hundred feet away, her features lit only by the campfire, but Lansing still did a double take. It looked just like Dr. Carerra to him.

The other woman turned her head. To Lansing she looked much younger than Carerra.

"I know her," Williston whispered anxiously.

"Which one?" the sheriff asked.

"The one on the left. The young one. That's Bets McGaffrey."

"Merrill McGaffrey's daughter?" Lansing asked, surprised. "What would she be doing up here?" The thought also passed through his mind, Why would Dr. Carerra be there?

"I don't know," Williston said. "Unless that third man brought her. Brought both of them."

"Or they somehow stumbled into this place," Lansing guessed. "Which I would find hard to believe. Whatever the case, it doesn't look like they were welcome." He paused for a moment. "We need to get them out of there."

"What?" Williston was surprised. "What do you mean?"

"We already know these jokers mean business. They've tried to kill a senator and a sheriff. A couple of women won't mean anything to them."

"Wouldn't we be better off trying to make it to town and get help?"

"Senator, there are no guarantees we'd make it to town. They have horses. We don't. They could track us down before we got out of the mountains. And even if we did get to town, I don't know that we'd make it back in time. These guys don't seem to be the type who'd wait around to be arrested. If they decide to run, the women would just slow them down. We need to do something now."

"What are we supposed to do? Walk down there and tell them to surrender?"

"The last thing they'd expect is for us to come after them."

"I'll go along with that," Williston commented. "It's the last thing I would come up with. They're the ones with the guns, Lansing. Remember?"

"We have weapons."

Williston gave him a strange look.

"In the caverns back there," Lansing explained. "There are hundreds of them."

"Those bows and arrows you were talking about!" Williston asked in disbelief. "I haven't shot archery in thirty years."

"What we don't have in accuracy we'll make up for with the element of surprise."

"You're nuts, Sheriff."

"I will help," Windwalker said, after listening to their arguments in silence.

"There you go, Senator. Three against three. The odds are even now."

"Lansing, listen to me. I can't shoot a bow and arrow."

Lansing scooted away from the edge of the cliff and stood. "Can you throw a baseball?"

"Certainly," Williston snorted. "You want me to throw rocks?"

"No, but if you can throw a baseball halfway accurately, you can use an atlatl."

"Atlatl?" the senator asked.

"Spear launcher. It will take you about five minutes to learn how to handle it. From up here it will be just as deadly and accurate as a rifle."

"I still say you're nuts, Lansing," Williston growled,

getting to his feet. "And I'm just as bad because I'm going along with it."

"We don't have much time. They'll probably stay right there till daybreak. We'll attack at first light."

## 35

CARERRA WOKE WITH A START. SHE HAD DOZED ON AND OFF for over an hour. It was still night. The man they called Hatch was still asleep a few feet away. Elizabeth was asleep as well. The fire was no more than embers and she felt a chill ripple through her.

The sound of approaching footsteps drew her attention to the canyon behind her. Parker and Reid ignored her as they walked past. Reid set down his carbine and started tossing twigs and sticks onto the dying fire. Parker walked over and kicked Hatch's foot.

Hatch was not a light sleeper. He mumbled something in his sleep but did not move. Parker kicked him again, harder. Hatch jerked awake.

"What?" he asked angrily.

"You'd make a piss-poor watchdog," Parker snapped.

"What am I supposed to watch for? There's nothing going on."

"You were supposed to make sure no one got through the tunnel over there."

"No one did," Hatch growled defensively. "What'd you find down the canyon?"

"Not a damned thing," Reid said from next to the

fire he was building. "If you ask me, they're halfway to Las Palmas by now."

"No one asked you," Parker commented.

Carerra pretended to still be asleep. She couldn't help but notice all three of her captors sounded tired and edgy. She hoped in their fatigue they'd make a mistake.

"What do we do now?" Hatch asked, approaching the fire to get warm.

"We couldn't pick up a trail in the dark," Parker explained. "But it doesn't look like there's a way out of this canyon. We'll take a look in the morning. If they did climb out, they'll be on foot. We can track them down easy enough."

Hatch lowered his voice and approached Parker. "What about those two?" He gestured toward the women with his thumb.

"They could serve a purpose. Williston took a shine to the young lady. We can use her to draw him out."

"After that?"

"We don't need any witnesses. Understand?"

"Yeah, I understand. . . . I just don't like the thought of killing women."

"Have Reid do it. He'll enjoy it." Parker turned away and spoke in a louder voice. "I'm going to check on the horses."

Carerra could catch only a few of the words that passed between Parker and Hatch. Both men kept looking in her direction during the discussion. She suspected they had a problem concerning what to do with her and Elizabeth.

When Parker left, Hatch signaled Reid to come over. As Hatch explained things, Reid looked first at Elizabeth, then at Carerra. The smile on Reid's face sent an uncontrollable shudder through the doctor's body.

Reid saw that Carerra was awake. When he finished

his conversation with Hatch, he walked over and knelt next to her.

"Ya know, pretty lady, you and I got off on the wrong foot. But ya know what? You ain't so bad lookin'. I don't know what those other guys got planned for you, but that doesn't mean you and I can't be friendly toward each other."

Carerra felt a wave of nausea at the thought of the man touching her. She suppressed the thought. "You know what," she responded coyly, "I think you're right. I know you were a little rough with me, but . . . I like that kind of thing."

"Oh, yeah!" Reid smiled broadly. There was a hunger in his eyes for the helpless woman in front of him.

"Listen," Carerra said, almost in a whisper. "It's quiet. It's dark. Let's get away from the light where we can be alone. . . . When you shoved me around . . . man, I really wanted you. I want you now."

Reid wiped saliva from the corner of his mouth as he looked back at Hatch. Hatch was smoking a cigarette, staring down at the empty canyon. He looked eagerly back at Carerra.

"Yeah. Yeah, I knew you'd like it. Real women like it rough." He began working on the knots around her ankles.

"What about the other two?" Carerra whispered.

"What about 'em?" Reid was so excited over the prospect of taking her, he couldn't concentrate on the knots.

"They're not going to let you. . . . They're not going to let us do it. . . ." She tried to sound worried.

"They can't stop us!" Reid said angrily.

"They're not going to let you untie me so I can have you."

"I can do any goddamn thing I want, and they can't stop me." Reid pulled out a hunting knife and cut through the leg ropes.

"Hurry," Carerra pleaded. "God, I want you."

Reid quickly scooted around to her back. He roughly grabbed her arms and began to cut at the rope.

"Hey!" Hatch bellowed. "What the hell do you think you're doing?"

Reid looked up. His face read anxiety and guilt, like a first-time shoplifter caught in the act. "None o' your business, Hatch."

"Get away from those ropes," Hatch said, approaching.

"Stay back. Me an' the lady are havin' a private conversation."

"See, I told you they wouldn't let us do anything," Carerra said anxiously.

"Shut up, bitch," Reid growled. He stood, the knife ready to be used as a weapon. "Me and the lady are going for a walk, an' there's not a damned thing you can do about it."

Hatch leveled his rifle at Reid. "I said leave the ropes alone."

"What the hell do you care? I'm just gonna have a little fun. I hate to see a good piece of tail go to waste."

"Just wait till Parker gets back. If he says it's okay, I don't care what you do."

"They're not going to let us," Carerra whispered.

"I'll take care of this," Reid said under his breath. "All right, all right," he said loudly, slipping his knife back into its sheath. "I can wait."

He stepped away from Carerra and started walking away from the fire. Hatch lowered the rifle and began to turn away. That's when Reid tackled his companion.

Hatch was definitely the smaller of the two. He managed to roll onto his back and tried to kick Reid away. The big man pushed Hatch's feet aside and pounced on his chest. Hatch tried desperately to protect himself as Reid began pounding him in the face and head with his fists.

"Reid!" Hatch screamed. "Get the hell off me!"

"Ain't no way you gonna tell me what to do!" Reid snarled. "You understand me? No way."

The rifle shot exploded the relative silence of the canyon. Reid stopped with his fist raised above his head. He looked in the direction of the tunnel.

Parker stood with his rifle pointed at Reid. "Get off him!" Parker barked.

Hatch pushed Reid away.

"What the hell's going on?" Parker demanded, his rifle leveled at the two men on the ground.

"Aw, we're just havin' a friendly disagreement," Reid said with a smile. "You know how it is, Parker."

Hatch had scurried a few feet away, grabbing his own rifle when he did. He pointed the gun at Reid. "Friendly, my ass," he wheezed, spitting blood. "I ought to blow your head off."

Parker kept his gun pointed at Reid. "What happened?"

"He decided he wanted a piece of ass," Hatch explained, wiping the blood from his nose. "I caught him trying to cut the ropes on that one." He gestured toward Carerra with his gun. "When I told him to wait till you got back, he jumped me."

"Reid?" Parker asked, looking for corroboration.

"She said she wanted it." The big man shrugged. "What am I gonna do? Pass it up?"

Parker lowered his rifle and walked close. "You stupid ass. She doesn't want you. You're not her type." Swinging his rifle, he caught Reid alongside his head with the barrel, knocking him to the ground. Reid grabbed at the growing welt on his face. "When there's work to do, that's all you're paid to worry about. Understand?"

"Yeah," Reid said weakly.

Parker walked over to Carerra to check the ropes around her wrists. They were still secure. "Nice try, honey. Almost got yourself untied. . . ." He slapped her across the face. "Tell you what. After we take care of business in the morning, if you want it so bad, I'll make sure you get it."

Parker raised his hand to hit her again. Carerra involuntarily recoiled to avoid the strike.

Parker laughed. "Good. I see we understand each other." He stood and walked away.

"What were you trying to do?" Elizabeth whispered, having watched the entire scene.

"Trying to make a break for it." Carerra frowned. "Didn't do a very good job, either."

"We'll get out of this somehow." Elizabeth tried to sound encouraging.

"I know." Carerra smiled. "I know." She had her doubts. She could still feel the sting from the slap across her face.

# 36

LANSING LOOKED DOWN AT THE CANYON FLOOR. THERE WAS no movement in the camp below. A thin wisp of smoke curled upward from the almost-dead fire.

His view was partially blocked by the mask he wore. He wasn't sure why Windwalker insisted they should be in costume for the assault. All the old man said was, "It will make the few look like many."

Williston sat a few feet away. His head was bowed as if in prayer. Lansing suspected the man was sleeping. Lansing guessed they both had been up for most of the last twenty-four hours, except for the occasional nap. Lansing felt bone tired. And he knew Williston was in much worse shape.

The last three hours had been a mad scramble. The three of them had returned to the shaft entrance of the caverns. Williston stayed on the surface to haul things from below. Lansing and Windwalker brought dozens of spears and three spear launchers from the armory to the bottom of the shaft. Windwalker scrambled to the top of the chimney with a rope. Lansing was amazed at how nimble and energetic the old man was.

While Lansing tied equipment to the rope and Williston hauled it to the surface, Windwalker went back into the caverns. The old Zuni finally returned when the last of the weapons were being pulled to the outside. He was carrying two bundles, one under each arm. He told Lansing to climb up the shaft and send the end of the rope back down. After Lansing and Williston pulled the bundles to the top, Windwalker joined them.

The training session with the atlatls and spears took longer than Lansing had predicted. He had learned to use a spear launcher as a Boy Scout. There was more to the technique than he had remembered. Fortunately, Windwalker was an adept teacher. Within twenty minutes both Lansing and Williston felt confident with their new weapons.

The walk back to the promontory overlooking the canyon was tiring. Each man carried sixteen spears and an atlatl. The two white men had an additional burden of the mysterious bundles Windwalker had supplied.

There was the faintest hint in the east of the sky getting lighter when they reached their position. Windwalker unwrapped the two bundles they had brought with them.

Each pack contained a complete ceremonial costume. Lansing had seen similar outfits worn by Native American dancers during ritual celebrations.

"In the ancient times," Windwalker explained, "to fight against an enemy was a sacred occasion. To be victorious, a warrior had to be superior not only physically, but spiritually as well. To please the spirits of his clan and to gain their support in battle, a man would dress himself to resemble a demon. If the spirits were pleased, they would stand beside him in battle. It confused the enemy and they did not know who to fight. It could make the few look like many."

Lansing picked up the wooden mask lying in front of him. The eyes looked as though they were bulging from their sockets. The nose was flat. The mouth was turned down at the corners in a perpetual and hideous frown. The tongue, carved into the face of the mask, looked as though it hung from the mouth, its owner being choked to death.

In the right place and under the right circumstances, Lansing knew the mask could frighten him if he wasn't prepared. The rest of the costume consisted of grass leggings, a leather loin piece, and a robe made from skins and feathers. A cone-shaped grass headdress that fit onto the costume before the mask was in place completed the ensemble.

The separate pieces were held in place by leather straps.

Windwalker helped each man don his costume. They wore the disguises over their regular clothes, and Lansing dressed first. He tried to suppress the feeling that he looked ridiculous. He changed his mind when he saw Williston.

The senator had dressed with his back to Lansing. Once Windwalker secured the mask, Williston turned. He held an atlatl in one hand and a spear in the other. The cone shaped headdress made him appear eight feet tall. The demon mask looked particularly menacing in the waning moonlight. The overall effect was both impressive and frightening. Lansing was suddenly reminded of Beau Watson's story about the demons in the desert. The tale suddenly took on an air of validity.

"I will go now," Windwalker said.

"Where?" Lansing asked, shaking off the thoughts of Beau's demons.

"To prepare. Today is the solstice. On the calendar of the Human Beings the summer solstice was the Center of Time. All other points to be reckoned were determined by the sunrise. I must prepare. Today we do battle at the Center of Time, at the Center of all the Universe."

Lansing and Williston looked at each other but did not comment.

"When should we start?" Williston asked, checking the balance of the spear he was holding.

"When the chanting has ended, the battle will begin." Windwalker turned and began walking away.

"Where will you be?" Lansing asked.

"On the battle line, among the warriors," Windwalker said over his shoulder. A moment later he disappeared behind some rocks. Lansing couldn't fathom Windwalker's statement. What battle line? What warriors?

After the hurried preparation, time seemed to come to a halt for the sheriff. He checked the skies, he checked his watch, he checked the canyon below—anything to occupy his mind. Williston sat quietly with his head bowed.

Lansing inspected his stockpile of weapons. He had twenty-four spears. Williston had the same number. They each had a spare atlatl. They had taken positions thirty feet apart to give themselves some separation for when the shooting started. The sheriff found himself torn between wishing the sun would hurry up and hoping it didn't come up at all.

"You know, Lansing," Williston said, raising his head. "When the sun comes up, it will be at our back. We're going to be sitting ducks up here."

"Senator, are you always this cheery in the morning or just when you've been up all night?"

Williston stood and stretched. "It may have to do with dressing for Halloween a few months too early." He turned and looked at Lansing. "I'm too old to cry and too tired to laugh, Lansing, but you do look ridiculous."

"I was going to compliment you on what a frightening sight you made, Senator."

"It's just the bags under my eyes, Sheriff. They'll do that to people not used to seeing me this time of day."

"You're wearing a mask," Lansing said dryly. "I can't see your eyes."

"Makes it that much more frightening, doesn't it?" He picked up a spear and fitted it into the groove of the missile launcher. "Well, Windwalker. I've made my peace. I'm ready anytime you are."

## 37

THE FEW CLOUDS IN THE SKY BEGAN TO GLOW ORANGISH PINK from the rays of a sun still hiding below the horizon. The bottom of the canyon was gradually starting to brighten, but the gauzy twilight still gave everything a two-dimensional appearance.

Dr. Carerra drifted in and out of a light sleep. The fire had long since dwindled to mere embers, leaving her with a chill. An involuntary shudder lifted her to consciousness. She looked around the camp. Hatch still leaned against his rock, hat cocked over his eyes, the rifle across his lap. Reid was curled into a ball a few feet away, snoring loudly. Parker had dozed off near the entrance to the tunnel.

"Elizabeth?" the doctor whispered.

The younger woman stirred slowly. She looked at Carerra bleary-eyed. "Yes?"

"I wanted to see if you were all right."

"Yeah, I guess so." As she became more cognizant of her surroundings, Bets looked around. "Is it morning yet?"

"Pretty close."

With their hands tied behind their backs, both women had slept sitting up. Elizabeth tried to stretch, but the bindings made it impossible. "My hands are numb," she complained.

Carerra had hoped they might try untying each other, but she found that she had no feelings in her own fingers. She considered using the final embers of the fire to burn away the ropes on her ankles, but had no idea where she would run for help. She tried to bolster her own spirits by telling herself it was always darkest just before the dawn. The pragmatic side of her nature pointed out it was now dawn and things weren't looking very good.

From the cliff wall just above the two women a voice began to boom across the canyon.

*"I huehue pil Alacinawe tlatoa pa i Katcina. Hua nican i Pautiwa, i Kuaklo, i Koyemshi, i Pekwin hua Ahayuta."* As the final words were spoken, the first phrase could still be heard echoing down the canyon. There was a brief pause as the echoes died away, then the chant was repeated.

"What's that?" Elizabeth asked.

Carerra shook her head. "It's Native American. I recognize a couple of the words, but I don't know what he's saying."

Lansing and Williston both looked into the canyon when the chant began.

"Where's that coming from?" Williston asked.

Lansing first looked across to the canyon rim opposite them. Seeing no one, he looked into the canyon. In the growing light he could make out a figure standing on the rock shelf of the cliff dwelling. He pointed. "Down there."

The figure was dressed in ceremonial robes, headdress, and a mask. He stood near the edge of the cliff shelf, arms spread wide, palms facing the heavens. The cavernous overhang acted as a megaphone, amplifying the figure's voice tenfold.

"Windwalker?" the senator asked.

"It has to be. But I don't know how the hell he got down there."

The chant ended, fading down the canyon, then began again.

"What's he doing?" It was Lansing's turn to ask.

"He's calling for reinforcements."

"You know what he's saying?"

"It's like that dream I had with the *a'doshle.* I couldn't understand the words, but I knew what they meant. He's calling himself the oldest son of the ancestors and he's speaking to the ancient gods. He's asking the High Spirits and Demons to intercede on our behalf . . . and bring the War Gods to this place."

The chant ended a second time, then started again.

When the chant began, Parker was the first to stir. "What the hell's going on?" he barked.

Hatch pushed his hat above his eyes, unable to stifle a yawn. "I don't know," he managed to say finally. He stood and kicked Reid.

"What!" Reid sat up angrily. "What d'ya want?"

"Get up," Hatch snapped, checking his rifle. "Something's going on."

Reid clumsily got to his feet. He grabbed his hat from the ground and dusted himself off with it. Parker readied his own rifle as he scanned the canyon around him for the source of the intrusion.

Elizabeth and Carerra were craning their necks to look toward the speaker. They had arrived after dark and were unaware of the magnificent dwellings encased in the canyon wall above them. From where Carerra sat, she could see the roof of the overhanging sandstone, but none of the buildings. A lone figure dressed in ceremonial robes stood near the edge of the rock shelf fifty feet above her. The figure was the source of the chant.

It didn't take Parker long to spot the costumed figure above him. "Up by the cliff dwellings." He gestured with his rifle.

"Must be that crazy old Indian," Hatch said. "The one I told you about yesterday."

"What's he doin'?" Reid wondered.

"I don't know," Parker said, raising his rifle to take aim. "But he won't be doing it for long."

"Look out!" Carerra screamed, just as Parker pulled the trigger.

The echoing shot reverberated through the canyon, drowning out Windwalker's chant. Windwalker did not move. He continued the chant.

"Dammit, I hit him!" Parker shouted. He looked at his rifle, then raised it for a second shot. From the far end of the canyon came the rumble of thunder.

"Wait," Hatch intervened. "Which one are you shooting at? I see two of them up there."

Parker lowered his rifle. A strong breeze had started suddenly. He had to squint to look at the shelf. Twenty feet from the figure he had shot at stood a second figure, similarly dressed, standing in the same pose.

The sound of approaching thunder became louder. At the far end of the canyon a huge black-brown cloud began spilling over the canyon rim.

"Shoot them both!" Parker shouted.

"Which ones?" Reid bellowed. "There's three. . . . No, there's four of them up there!"

"Kill them all!" Parker raised his rifle and all three men began firing.

From the canyon rim the sheriff and senator watched the reactions in the camp. They couldn't hear the conversation between the men, but they heard Dr. Carerra's shout as Parker raised his rifle and fired.

Both men looked at Windwalker. The old Indian stood his ground and continued his chant.

Lansing raised the atlatl and was ready to launch a spear when Williston stopped him. "Wait till the chant's over."

"They're going to kill him!"

"Wait!" the senator ordered.

Lansing watched helplessly as all three men opened fire on the lone figure. For some strange reason, the gunmen were aiming wildly, their bullets striking feet, even yards away from Windwalker. The sheriff barely noticed the wind that had started tugging at his costume.

Windwalker's chant had increased in volume to overcome the wail of the wind. It sounded as though dozens of voices had joined in the tautology. From the canyon rim, though, Windwalker remained the sole figure on the rock shelf.

The old man raised his hands above his head, as if in a final appeal to the ancients. Suddenly the chanting stopped and the Watcher dropped his hands.

"Now!" Williston commanded as he launched his first spear.

# 38

DR. CARERRA WATCHED IN FASCINATION AS PARKER, HATCH, and Reid fired dozens of shots at the figures on the rock shelf. Despite the efforts of the gunmen, not one of the individuals fell. She tried to count how many there were, but the increasing wind made it difficult for her to see. There were more than six costumed forms on the ledge. How many more, she couldn't tell.

The howl of the wind was mixed with a cacophony of voices and rolling thunder. The growing light of the morning sun was rapidly being obscured by a cloud of sand and dust that filled the canyon.

Suddenly the chanting stopped. Carerra squeezed her eyes open to venture a look at the rock shelf above her. The figures had disappeared.

Something solid hit the ground next to her. She turned her head to see the shaft of a spear protruding from the ground not five feet from where she sat. A second missile embedded itself just a foot from where Reid stood.

"Look up there!" Reid screamed, pointing to the canyon rim.

Carerra tried to peer through the whirling maelstrom that had engulfed them. Silhouetted by the rising sun, dozens upon dozens of costumed figures with grotesque faces stood along the canyon rim. It was as if all the demons from hell had converged on that one spot. Each was armed with a spear. Once they hurled their weapon into the canyon they rearmed to launch a second, then a third. The crashing thunder and wailing wind made them sound like an army of thousands.

The three gunmen began to fire wildly at the canyon rim.

The rain of spears continued.

Hatch was the first to fall. A spear pierced his right thigh. He fell backward, shooting blindly at the top of the canyon. A second missile caught him square in the chest.

Reid had just loaded a new clip into his M-16 when Hatch screamed. The big man looked over to see his companion clutching desperately at the spear protruding from his upper torso.

"You bastards!" Reid bellowed above the tempest. He clicked the carbine to rapid-fire and began spraying the ledge above him. He never had time to react as the pike drove through his eye socket, through the back of his skull, and into the earth behind him. With Reid's finger frozen on the trigger, the M-16 continued to fire until the magazine was empty. The bullets bounced harmlessly off the canyon wall.

Williston's first spear went a little long and he shuddered when he saw it hit so close to the two women. He saw that Lansing's aim was significantly better. The lawman's first missile came within inches of his target.

Williston felt a pang of guilt. His sense of fair play suggested to him this surprise attack was like shooting a man in the back. His doubts were immediately squelched when the gunmen turned their fire on him.

The senator's second attempt was closer to his mark. He was aiming for Reid, his tormentor from the day before. He thought for sure the big man would take him out before he could mete out his revenge. Instead, Reid was shooting at something yards away from where Williston stood. Williston didn't argue. He simply continued to hurl his spears, each one getting closer to his target.

Williston saw Hatch fall, a spear sticking from his leg. Lansing had his trajectory down pat as he hurled another missile, impaling his target through the chest.

The senator was not to be outdone. As Reid clicked a new magazine into the M-16, Williston carefully aimed his weapon. Using his left arm as a guide, he concentrated on a spot between Reid's eyes. Reid pointed the weapon directly at Williston.

Williston put all his weight into the throw. Reid fired at the same moment. The senator never saw the shaft make its mark as he was thrown backward by the force of the bullet striking him.

Parker continued to fire at their attackers until his rifle was empty. He tried to shout above the gale. "Reid! Hatch!"

There was no response. There was no other gunfire either.

A spear ripped through Parker's shirtsleeve, shredding the material and slicing his arm open just below the shoulder. He screamed as he threw his rifle down.

"Reid! Hatch! Let's get the hell out of here!"

Turning to the tunnel, Parker tripped, falling face first. A spear embedded itself in the ground next to his head. Scrambling to his feet, Parker lunged through the entrance to the passageway and disappeared in the darkness.

# 39

LANSING SAW THE THIRD GUNMAN YELLING AT HIS COHORTS. It was obvious to the sheriff that the other two were dead. What the man was yelling about, he had no idea. He launched the spear he was holding.

The shaft ripped through the man's shirt but didn't seem to do much damage. Lansing picked up another spear. The last of the gunmen threw his rifle down and started running. Lansing led his quarry by two steps, then launched his missile. If the man hadn't tripped, the sheriff would have caught him square in the back.

The lawman picked up another shaft. Before he could launch it, the target had already disappeared into the tunnel. Lansing hurled the spear into the black opening anyway, in case the gunman had second thoughts about coming back.

"Senator, we did it!" Lansing turned to Williston. The senator lay motionless on the ground. "Oh, my God!" Lansing swore. He ripped the mask from his face as he ran toward his comrade in arms.

"Senator? Senator?" Lansing knelt next to the supine body. There was a single bullet hole in the mask, positioned between the two eyeholes. "Damn," Lansing growled, fumbling to get the mask off Williston. He finally managed to slip the disguise over the senator's head. It wasn't the bloody mess the sheriff had expected. In fact, there was no blood at all. Instead, there was a red dimple in the middle of Williston's forehead.

Lansing looked in the mask. The bullet protruded from the thick wood by an eighth of an inch.

The sheriff quickly checked him for other damage, but there was none. Williston had simply been knocked out cold. Lansing breathed a sigh of relief. As he stripped away his costume, Williston began regaining consciousness.

"What happened?" the senator asked thickly.

"You took a bump on the head, but I think you're going to be all right." He handed Williston the mask and showed him the bullet.

"What do you think?" Williston asked, rubbing the spot on his forehead. "Was it the mask or my skull that stopped it?"

"I'll leave that one for your political opponents to kick around. Right now, we need to get down to the canyon. Will you be all right?"

"Sure."

Lansing held out his hand and helped the senator to his feet.

Carerra tried to watch as much of the battle as she could, but the blowing sand made it nearly impossible. The wind, thunder, and rifle reports were deafening. Above it all she heard a man scream. Through the churning dust she saw Hatch with two spears protruding from his body.

A moment later the M-16 began spraying the rock wall in front of them. Then it suddenly quit. One rifle continued to fire for another minute, then it, too, was silenced.

She could barely make out Parker's voice above the

storm. He was yelling something to the other two. She heard "Hatch" and "Reid" but the rest was smothered in the wind. Parker quit yelling.

Then, as if someone had just closed a door, the wind stopped. The canyon began to brighten. From above her, somewhere on the canyon rim, someone called her name.

"Dr. Carerra . . . Margarite! Can you hear me?"

She stared into the bright, eastern sky. "Yes. Yes, I can. Who's there?" Not that she really cared. It sounded like a friendly voice.

"It's Cliff Lansing. Are you all right?"

"I'd be better if you'd untie me."

"Bets . . . This is Senator Williston. Are you okay?"

"Yes, Senator," Elizabeth called back, excitement in her voice. "Yes. I'm fine."

"You ladies hold on," Lansing yelled. "We'll be there as soon as we can."

Lansing didn't bother with trying to untie the ropes on Carerra and Elizabeth. He sawed through the hemp cords with ease. The sheriff was pleasantly surprised by Dr. Carerra's response. Once her hands were free, she put her arms around his neck and gave him the biggest kiss on the lips she could muster.

Williston got a similar response from Bets, only his kiss was on the cheek.

"What was that for?"

"Lansing, compared to what I thought I was going to wake up to this morning," she said, rubbing her wrists, "that's the least I could do. What'd you do with the rest of the cavalry?"

"What cavalry? What are you talking about?"

"You were up there on the ridge, weren't you?"

"Yeah."

"Well, where's the rest of them?"

Lansing and Williston looked at each other. They had no idea what she was talking about. "The rest of who?" the senator asked.

"It looked like there were at least a hundred warriors on the canyon rim."

"At least a hundred," Elizabeth confirmed. "It was hard to tell in the sandstorm."

Lansing looked at Elizabeth, then at Carerra. "Sandstorm?"

"Yes. Sandstorm," Carerra insisted, becoming irritated at not being believed. "I've lived in the desert all my life. I know a sandstorm when I see one."

"I apologize." Lansing backed down. "It was hard to see much in those masks . . . and from the rim up there, the canyon was still pretty dark."

The look on Carerra's face told Lansing he was forgiven.

"What about the others up there with you?" Bets asked.

"All I know is what Windwalker told us," Williston explained. "If the spirits were pleased with our costumes, they would make the few look like many."

"Speaking of Windwalker . . ." Lansing stood, helping Carerra to her feet. "Where is he?"

"Must still be up in the dwellings."

"What dwellings?" Carerra asked.

Lansing led her a few feet across the canyon so she could get a better view. All she could do was gasp. The rising sun was just beginning to illuminate the stone-and-mortar apartment dwellings. The small city looked as though it were constructed of gold.

"Senator, if you can handle that climb to see if you can find Windwalker, I'll see if there are any horses left."

"I can handle it."

Lansing found his pistol in Reid's belt. As Williston

made one last climb up the rock face, Lansing headed for the tunnel and the outer canyon. Dr. Carerra accompanied him.

To find Windwalker, all Williston had to do was follow the trail of blood. It started near the edge of the shelf. There was a large pool of dark red liquid where Windwalker had been standing. The trail led directly to the entrance of the grand kiva, the ceremonial chamber Williston had entered the day before.

The senator shook his head at the thought: the day before. It seemed like a lifetime ago.

In the dim light of the kiva, Williston found Windwalker lying on the clay floor. He still wore the ceremonial costume. The senator carefully removed the headdress and mask. Windwalker was still breathing, but barely. Williston opened the front of the blood-soaked costume. There were two bullet holes in the chest.

Williston stood to leave. He needed to get help.

"Senator Carter Williston," the *Kiaklo* whispered.

Williston returned to his side. "Don't talk. I'm going to get help."

"It is too late for that," the Watcher said. "It is past my time. I am ready to join the *Alacinawe,* the ancestors. It is time for the Children of the *Shipap* to return home."

"I will see that they do."

"That is good," Windwalker whispered. "The *a'doshle* were wise in choosing you, Senator Williston. . . . We will meet again . . . on the other side." The words faded to practically nothing, followed by a faint rattle from the Watcher's chest. The last sound was a gurgle as the final breath escaped the old man's body. Williston covered the Indian with the ceremonial robe.

"Was he your friend?" a soft voice asked.

Williston turned to find Bets McGaffrey standing at the bottom of the ladder. The senator nodded. "Yes, he was my friend . . . and a lot more."

## 40

LANSING REMEMBERED THE JOURNEY BACK TO LAS PALMAS more as a dream than as an experience.

He had planned on sending a party to recover the bodies. Williston insisted that the inner canyon be kept a secret until he had talked with the Zuni Tribal Council. Windwalker was left in the kiva. The bodies of Hatch and Reid were dragged into the outer canyon, then covered with rocks to protect the remains from vultures and coyotes.

Once the mortuary details were completed, the two men and two women headed back to civilization. Parker had left Cement Head and the other two horses behind, presumably for his colleagues to use. Elizabeth and Margarite shared one horse. Lansing and Williston each had their own.

The sheriff was grateful to find Joe Cortez waiting for them at Lansing's truck. The deputy had already organized a search party and was waiting for them to assemble when Lansing and his company arrived.

They were all surprised to find out Cortez was only looking for Lansing. No one had reported Williston, Elizabeth, or Dr. Carerra missing. When Cortez called back to Marilyn, Lansing insisted that he mention nothing about the others.

Lansing loaded Cement Head into the trailer and drove back to town with Dr. Carerra. He wanted to get her alone to find out how she had ended up in the mountains as a prisoner. It took some prying, but she finally admitted she was worried about him. He tried to brush off her concern with bravado, but deep inside he found the idea that someone could care for him again very warming. She filled him in on the details of her and Elizabeth's adventures: Longtree's body in the adobe hut, the mystery gunman who fired at them, the encounter with Cement Head, their capture by Parker and company.

Deputy Cortez took Williston and Elizabeth in his car. The other two horses were tied to a scrub bush. Joe asked Marilyn to dispatch someone to retrieve them before it got too hot.

On the way back to town, Elizabeth wanted to talk. Williston did his best to hold a conversation, but exhaustion was taking its toll. Despite his best efforts, the senator kept nodding to sleep. When they parked next to the courthouse, Williston's head was in Bets's lap. It took several minutes to rouse him to the point that he could get out of the patrol car.

It was noon when Lansing finally walked into his offices. He hung his holster on the coatrack and absentmindedly checked his pockets for any extra items. He found the shell casings from the cliff dwelling and the piece of pottery from the scene of Duke Semple's murder. He tossed the items onto his desk and forgot about them.

Las Palmas was too small a town to keep a secret for very long. Until he could sort it all out, the sheriff wanted to keep a lid on things.

With their permission, Lansing had beds set up in the day room for Elizabeth and Dr. Carerra. By that point they were grateful for any semisoft place to lie down. Whatever happened, Elizabeth had no intention of going home.

Beau Watson had been sprung, so the sheriff let Williston enjoy the comfort of one of the cells. Williston would have been satisfied with the concrete floor.

Since Joe Cortez had already found an adequate number of men to handle a search party, he was dispatched to retrieve the bodies from the Anasazi Strip. Lansing pinpointed the location of the outer canyon on the map. Stu Ortega was told to check out the small adobe hut at the far end of the strip. If there was a body there, he was to leave it alone. They would go out there for forensic samples in the morning.

Despite his misgivings, the sheriff had Deputy Peters called into the office. He knew he was stretching his resources, but he had to act quickly.

While the others slept, Lansing had Marilyn pick up some women's clothing at Beacon's. The sheriff himself headed home for a shower. When he returned an hour later, he brought some clothes for Williston. The two men were close enough in size that the shirt and pants would suffice for the interim.

Stu Ortega was already back from the adobe hut. Lansing was surprised. Ortega had never been noted for his ability to get anything done expeditiously. His report wasn't encouraging. Someone had set fire to the hut and the two Jeeps outside. From what the deputy could tell, there was no body in the ashes of the hut.

Despite the fact someone was destroying evidence, it was only a minor setback. For Lansing, the foreman of the McGaffrey ranch was going to be the key.

By three o'clock things were falling into place. The state police had delivered the special equipment Lansing had asked for and he had an arrest warrant in hand for Parker: attempted murder. At that point no one was sure who killed Windwalker. But the sheriff had been an eyewitness to Parker's at least trying to kill the man. That was good enough for the judge.

Williston was the first to stir. He cleaned up in the jail shower and donned the borrowed clothes. For the first time in years he asked for coffee with caffeine. With Lansing's permission he sequestered himself in the sheriff's private office to make some phone calls.

Marilyn brought in meals from the diner. The aroma was sufficient to rouse Elizabeth and Dr. Carerra. The two women ate voraciously before taking turns in the shower.

As Elizabeth sat on a cot in the day room brushing her hair out to dry, there was a knock at the door. "Come in," she said through the veil of hair.

Williston entered the room, closing the door behind him. "Hi, Bets. How are you feeling?"

"Clean, finally," she said with a laugh.

"Do you mind if I sit down?"

"No, please do."

Williston sat on a chair next to a desk. "I know you tried to tell me this morning why you went up to the strip. I wasn't a very good listener. Would you mind telling me again?"

"Sure," she said, noticing the serious tone of his voice. "My father was talking to someone on the phone. Someone from your office, I think. At breakfast you said you'd be back sometime yesterday afternoon. My father was telling this person you wouldn't be back for two days. . . . I tried to find you to make sure you were all right."

Williston stared at the floor thoughtfully for a moment before looking at the young lady. "Thank you. If you and Dr. Carerra hadn't shown up, I doubt if Sheriff Lansing and I would have made it back to town. . . . I don't know how to tell you this, other than come right out with it. I don't think your father planned on me coming back."

Elizabeth stared at him with a very noncommittal expression. Finally she said, "I don't think so, either, Senator. That's why I had to find you. Mack McGaffrey has just about destroyed everything in my life. I couldn't let him destroy you too."

Williston tried to smile, but it was halfhearted. The senator had come to the same conclusion about McGaffrey. He would destroy anybody and anything that got in his way. McGaffrey was the Destroyer. He had traced the legends of the Zuni people back to their Anasazi fathers, the Ancient Ones. He knew he had found the *Shipap,* or that it was at least close by. He wanted it for himself, not because of its religious or mystical significance, but for the money he could make from plundering its archeological wealth. If he destroyed an entire people and their culture at the same time, it didn't matter.

"Thanks." Williston stood and went to the door. He stopped with his hand on the knob. "I just wanted you to know, the sheriff and I are going after him. Parker isn't smart enough to pull off the murder of a U.S. senator. He was just doing what he was told to do."

"Senator, when the sheriff arrests him," Elizabeth said, staring at the floor, "tell him his daughter hopes he burns in hell." She looked up at Williston with tears in her eyes. "Could you do that, please?"

Williston could only nod. Whatever her hurt was, she had borne it for a long time. He hoped this final episode would end her pain. Opening the door, he left the room.

# 41

MACK MCGAFFREY SAT QUIETLY IN HIS STUDY TRYING TO FIT the final pieces of the ancient bowl together. He didn't look up when there was a knock at the door. "Yes?" he asked, totally absorbed in his work.

Ramón opened the door. "Señor McGaffrey. There is a Mr. Harding here to see you. He says he is from Senator Williston's office."

McGaffrey thought for a moment, then set down the pottery shards he was holding. "Yeah, show him in."

Ramón left. A moment later Harding showed up at the door to the study.

"Come in, Harding," McGaffrey said, walking around to the front of his desk. He ignored Harding's extended hand. "What brings you up here? I told you yesterday I didn't expect the senator back until tomorrow."

"There seems to be a problem, Mr. McGaffrey. The senator's not coming back."

"Oh?" There was a touch of concern in the rancher's voice.

"Yes," Harding said, taking a seat, even though it wasn't offered. "I got a call from the San Phillipe County sheriff's office this afternoon. It seems somebody found Carter Williston's body up on the Anasazi Strip this morning. They called my office first thing. . . . You know, publicity control and all that. They also needed somebody to come up here and identify the body."

"My God." McGaffrey shook his head. "Was it Williston's body?"

"I don't know," Harding admitted. "I haven't gone to the funeral home yet. They're not expecting me for another hour."

"What are you doing here?" McGaffrey asked suspiciously.

"You could say I'm taking care of damage control."

"How so?"

"Two days ago the senator asked me to look into why the secretary of the interior rolled over so readily on the Anasazi land-swap proposal. Secretary Milton seems clean enough. He turned all his financial holdings over to his brother-in-law to manage while Milton does his public duty. It's interesting, though. The holding company the brother-in-law runs has made a tremendous amount of money by investing in new-issue stocks."

"The man should be congratulated," McGaffrey said, trying to sound bored.

"All the new-issue stocks are in one way or another affiliated with McGaffrey Industries."

"An astute investor."

"Maybe so," Harding admitted. "And worst case scenario, the secretary can claim coincidence. Though there is one suspicious element in all this. The Bureau of Land Management has an addendum to the environmental impact study. It already has Secretary Milton's signature on it. It says the Anasazi Strip is going on public sale . . . and that McGaffrey Industries has already negotiated a 'fair market price' for the entire parcel."

"I don't know what you're talking about."

"I have a photocopy of the addendum in a safe-deposit box in Washington. I can fax you a copy if you want. It might jog your memory."

"What's your game, Harding?"

"Williston and some crazy old Indian were the only two people standing between you and the Anasazi Strip. I don't know about the Indian, but Williston's dead. The sheriff's office thought he was killed by a gunshot, but they're not sure. The body was pretty banged up.

"It's a federal crime to assassinate a U.S. senator. You're the only one around who'd profit from Williston's death."

"I still don't know what you're driving at."

"Autopsies can be doctored. Coroners can be paid off. Senator Williston could have died from a fall. That's pretty rugged terrain out there."

"And what's your price?"

"You're the power broker in this state. I want to be appointed as interim senator. Next year, I want your full support when election time rolls around."

"What do I get out of all this?"

"You get the Anasazi Strip. I squelch any investigations. You get my silence. I get your support. A very clean deal."

McGaffrey smiled and nodded as he walked around to the back of his desk. "I like deals, Harding. I like to think of myself as a master of the deal. To be a master at it, you have to make sure everything is lined up in your favor.

"This deal stinks. You'd have something to hang over my head for the rest of my life."

"I wouldn't use that against you."

"Why not? If I were in your shoes, I would." McGaffrey reached into his desk drawer and pulled out a pistol. "I can get autopsies doctored without your help.

I've done it before. I can pay off my own coroners. Right now, the only thing that's standing between me and the Anasazi Strip is you. It took a little effort to get rid of Williston. You won't be any problem at all."

"You're not going to shoot me here, are you?" Harding stood nervously.

"Oh, yes I am. But they'll find your body at some rest stop between Las Palmas and Santa Fe. People get killed in those places all the time." He fired.

"Drop it!" Lansing shouted from the doorway, his Magnum pointed at McGaffrey.

Without thinking, McGaffrey turned to aim at Lansing. Both men fired at once. The bullet meant for Lansing's head embedded in the doorjamb. McGaffrey's throat exploded from the impact of the .357 caliber projectile.

Williston rushed past the sheriff to Harding. The senator's assistant was trying to get to his feet. He was bleeding profusely from the bullet wound to his left shoulder. Williston helped him into a chair.

"Damn, Carter! You didn't tell me he was going to shoot me!"

"Harding, I'm sorry. I had no idea." The senator looked at the wound. "Ramón," he bellowed, "get us some towels in here! Pronto!"

"I'd better get a goddamn raise for this." Harding winced.

"At least that, buddy. At least that."

Lansing checked on McGaffrey. The millionaire rancher was dead. The sheriff picked up the phone and dialed a quick series of numbers. While he talked on the phone, Ramón rushed in with a handful of towels. Williston began putting pressure to the wound.

"Yeah, Peters. Sheriff Lansing. I need a medevac up to the McGaffrey ranch. They can use the private field up here. . . . Yes, dammit, it is an emergency. Gunshot wound. Tell them we don't know how serious. . . . And get me an ambulance up here. I have another body for the funeral home. . . . No, just do it!" Lansing slammed the receiver down. "If I could find a replacement, I'd fire him in a minute," he complained under his breath.

The sheriff came over to Harding. "I'm sorry we didn't get in here quicker."

"Yeah," Harding complained. "Me too . . . Did you get it all down on tape?"

"Sure did." Lansing nodded. "The state police were a little reluctant in loaning the equipment to us. They don't trust small-town sheriffs." He patted Harding on his good shoulder. "You did a great job. Just hang in there. Hopefully, it won't be too long."

The sheriff walked back over to the phone and dialed again. "Marilyn, this is Cliff. Is Dr. Carerra still there? Sure, I'll hold." He absentmindedly played with the pottery shards McGaffrey had been working with on his desk. They seemed vaguely familiar to him, but he couldn't understand why. "Yes, I'm still here," he said when Marilyn returned. "Oh, she left already? No, that's okay. If she calls from her clinic, tell her I'll try to reach her later. Thanks."

"What about Parker?" Williston asked, still tending to his aide.

"There's an APB out on him. All we can do is hope he turns up somewhere." From outside the ranch house came the sound of a gunshot. "Wait here!" Lansing ordered, drawing his gun while he ran from the room.

From the patio, he saw Stu Ortega emerging from the stables. The deputy was holding a pistol. Lansing ran to him.

"What the hell's going on?" the sheriff asked, almost out of breath.

"I—I found Parker hiding in the stables," the deputy said nervously. "He said he'd pay me if I let him go. I told him no, I couldn't do that. So he pointed a gun at me and I shot him."

Lansing rushed into the stables. Parker lay facedown on the dirt floor. The sheriff checked the neck for a pulse but couldn't find one. Rolling the body over, there was a single gunshot wound to the chest. He walked back outside to where his deputy stood.

"He's dead," Lansing reported. He could see Ortega was shaking like a leaf. The sheriff carefully took the pistol from the deputy. "First time you ever shot a man, isn't it?"

"Yeah, I guess." Ortega nodded.

"Come on up to the house. We could both use a drink."

Lansing really did need a drink. It was over. He couldn't believe how quickly and cleanly it had ended. There'd be a lot of follow-up reports he'd have to file with the state. There was still the matter of trying to figure out what Parker had done with Longtree's body. But for the most part it was over and Lansing was glad.

# 42

Las Palmas was sheer chaos for the first week after McGaffrey's death. Williston's withdrawal of the proposed Anasazi Strip land swap made regional news. The death of multimillionaire Merrill McGaffrey at the hands of law officers made national news. The assassination attempt against a U.S. senator made international news. For an entire week schoolchildren could find New Mexico on a map.

Las Palmas was inundated by news media of all type. The streets were clogged with television vans equipped with direct satellite hookups to their home stations. So much power was drained from the local co-op, there were three brownouts in the first two days.

Velma and Kelly basked in the limelight of so many personal interviews, they almost lost their jobs at the diner. As it was, the owner had to bring in part-time help to handle the overflow of customers. Velma was so busy flirting with television reporters, she forgot all about Dr. Tanner, at least for the time being.

Williston did his best to protect Elizabeth McGaffrey from the onslaught of reporters. When Lansing had garnered all the information he needed for his investigation, he helped the senator sneak her out of town. Only Lansing and Williston knew she was staying with Williston's wife in Baltimore.

As far as the plot against Williston went, Elizabeth had very little to offer. On the tape Harding had helped secure, McGaffrey made reference to having doctored autopsy reports before. Elizabeth had her day in court when she recounted the death of her mother. She maintained her father had been responsible and had paid off investigators to clear his name. The governor of New Mexico pledged his full support in reopening the case of the alleged suicide of Elizabeth's mother.

Senator Williston managed to keep the mystery buried in the Anasazi Strip a secret for a few days. He flew the Zuni Tribal Council to Las Palmas and personally escorted them to the cliff dwelling and the *Shipap*. No reporters were allowed, even though several media helicopters tried to follow them. The tribal members were beyond words in trying to express their gratitude to Williston and the federal government.

One tribal elder was eventually overcome by media pressure and bragged about the great heritage of the Human Beings finally unveiled to them. The National Guard had to be dispatched to keep out the plunderers and the curious alike.

Before Williston headed back to Washington, Lansing managed to corner him for a private conversation.

"Senator," Lansing asked in the isolation of his office, "I hate to sound like a skeptic, but what did you see up on the strip?"

"What did you see, Lansing?"

"To be perfectly honest, I didn't see a damned thing. I didn't see a hundred warriors standing on the canyon rim with us. I didn't see the dozen Windwalkers next to the cliff dwelling chanting for the gods. I didn't see spirits sweeping through the caverns to bring you back to the land of the living. I never saw the bogeyman that scared the hell out of Beau Watson. What did you see?"

"I've been a pragmatist all my life," the senator said thoughtfully. "My pragmatic side tells me I saw what Windwalker wanted me to see. He was a master illusionist . . . a shaman."

"What does your unpragmatic side tell you?"

"My unpragmatic side tells me I saw everything I thought I saw . . . including my own soul.

"I've spent a lifetime worrying what price each man has. I always kidded myself that I was above all that. I wasn't. I wanted power, although I managed to bury the desire under more altruistic motives. To get it I sold my soul to Mack McGaffrey. Windwalker showed me the road to redemption.

"I don't know if you believe in the *a'doshle* or the power of the *Shipap*. It doesn't matter. I do." He stood and extended his hand. "Thanks, Lansing. Thanks for everything."

Lansing shook Williston's hand warmly. "Anytime, Senator. Anytime . . . You will be back this way, won't you?"

"You can count on it, Sheriff." Williston opened the door and left.

The dinner with Dr. Carerra came a week later than Lansing had planned. They avoided the diner. The cantina was darker, more private, and it served beer.

"You know what I can't understand, Lansing," Carerra said after finishing her dinner. "How did Parker get from the adobe hut all the way to the canyon so fast?"

"What do you mean?" the sheriff asked, taking a sip of beer.

"I read Senator Williston's interview in the paper. He said that he and Windwalker rode for almost three hours from the hut until they reached the canyon of the *Shipap*. It took Elizabeth and me at least that long.

"It was just getting dark when we were shot at. You said that you climbed down from the dwelling right after dark."

"Yes." Lansing nodded, trying to follow her logic.

"And you said Parker was already there."

"Yeah, he was. We heard him yell at Hatch and Reid."

"How could it have been Parker shooting at us if he was at the canyon?"

Lansing leaned back in his seat, thinking. "McGaffrey?"

"I know he was a bastard," Carerra admitted, "but I don't think he would have shot his daughter. Besides, how would he know where to find her?"

"Holy cow," Lansing whispered. He lost himself with his own thoughts for a moment.

"Lansing." Carerra waved her hand in front of his face. "You still there?"

The sheriff sat up suddenly. "I hate to do this to you, but I have to get back to my office."

"And do what?" the doctor asked indignantly.

"I have to look into something," he said, an edge of agitation to his voice. He stood and threw a twenty-dollar bill on the table to cover dinner.

"You're not going anywhere without me!" Carerra insisted. "If you're going to find out who shot at me, I'm coming. And you can't stop me."

"All right, come on."

The two left the cantina.

Deputy Peters was on the phone when Lansing and Carerra entered the office.

"Hold on, Momma. Sheriff Lansing just came in." He pulled the phone away from his face. "Can I help you, Sheriff?"

"Yes," Lansing said, pulling the phone from Peters's hand and slamming it down on the cradle. "Last week when I was up on the strip, Dr. Carerra and Elizabeth McGaffrey came in here."

"Yes, sir," Peters said, trying not to pout. "I remember."

"Did you tell anyone they were heading to the strip?"

"No." Peters's face brightened. "But I can check my logbook." He opened the dispatch log Marilyn kept. Deputy Peters's one sterling attribute was that he logged every incoming call he got and radio dispatch he made. "Let me see. June twentieth. Deputy Cortez radioed in at six-thirty. I told him they had driven down to the strip to see if they could find you."

"What time did he finally get in here?"

"About eight-thirty."

"What about Stu?"

"He got in about nine."

"Where had he been?"

"Santa Fe. Remember, you sent him down with the forensic samples?"

"Yeah, yeah." Lansing went into his office, followed by Carerra.

"What now?" Margarite asked.

"I don't know." He sat sullenly at his desk. "Somebody could have picked up that call on a scanner. Anybody could have followed you there."

The top of his desk was a mess. There were scraps of paper with phone numbers from reporters, a cigar wrapper, even the shell casings he'd picked up at the cliff dwelling. He picked up his trash can and began sweeping the debris into it. One out-of-place item caught his eye: a small piece of pottery.

He picked it up and examined it, then looked at Carerra. "You up for a little drive?"

"Sure."

Lansing pulled his holster from the coatrack and strapped it on. A few minutes later they were speeding out of town, toward the McGaffrey ranch.

Ramón answered the door when Lansing knocked. The cook and most of the ranch hands were still on the ranch to run things, although the wheels were already in motion in probate court.

Lansing asked to see the study. Ramón led them to the darkened part of the house. The room was still roped off with yellow crime-scene tape. Lansing pushed through it and turned on the light.

The room had not been touched since the previous week. Even McGaffrey's lawyers had not been given access to his personal safe yet.

The sheriff walked directly to the desk. The pottery shards he had toyed with a week earlier were still where he left them. He sat at the desk and pulled a piece of pottery from his pocket.

"What are you doing?"

"Seeing if these match." He compared the fire-hardened glaze exterior of his piece to several pieces on the table. They were identical. He rearranged the pieces two or three times until the shard from his office fit perfectly with the puzzle on the desk.

Lansing picked up the phone and called his office. "Peters, this is Sheriff Lansing. I want you to call up Joe Cortez and Stu Ortega. . . . Yes, I know it's after hours. I want you to tell them to meet me at the spot we found Duke Semple's body. . . . No, I don't think they'll get lost. . . . No! I don't care who drives. Just tell them to be there!" He slammed the receiver down.

He looked Carerra squarely in the face. "One of these days I really am going to fire him . . . if I don't kill him first."

The deputies were already waiting for Lansing and Carerra when they pulled up.

"What's up, Chief?" Stu asked as Lansing got out of his Jeep.

"We're going to do some police work," Lansing said. He opened the back of his Jeep and pulled out two shovels. Dr. Carerra got out from her side of the Jeep carrying two flashlights.

He handed each deputy a shovel. "Grab your flashlights. We're going to take a little walk."

Taking a flashlight from Carerra, Lansing started leading them toward a low ridge. The moon was less than half full and provided very little light.

"What are we doing?" Joe asked, using his light to pick his way between bushes.

"You know how we've had a boger of a time trying to figure out where Parker hid Longtree's body?"

"Yeah," Joe admitted. "We used bloodhounds and everything. Couldn't find nothing."

"The bloodhounds couldn't do us any good because there wasn't a scent to follow. That's why they burned up the hut and the Jeeps. . . . Also gets rid of fingerprints."

"Ah-ha," Stu said. "That makes sense."

"Anyway, I think we've been looking in the wrong place all along."

They descended the hill to a low, flat plain. The moon gave enough light for them to see the pale outline of an abandoned village.

Lansing walked directly to the circle outlining the kiva. He flashed his light around until he found the spot he wanted. There was a pattern of disturbed earth at the very center of the circle. He pointed at the spot with his flashlight. "I want you boys to dig here."

"Okay." Joe shrugged. They both began digging.

"Joe," Lansing asked, "when you talked to Peters last week—the night I was stuck out here—why didn't you follow Dr. Carerra and Miss McGaffrey down to the strip to help look for me?"

"Me?" Joe stopped digging. "I was still up in North County. I was trying to break up a family fight. I didn't get back till almost eight-thirty. I figured they'd give up and come home. Besides, you said you could take care of yourself."

Lansing nodded and Cortez went back to digging.

"Stu?"

"Yes, sir." Ortega looked up.

"Where were you?"

"Ah," he said sheepishly. "You sent me down to Santa Fe. I had to take the stuff into the crime lab. You remember."

"Yeah, I also remember telling you to get right back here when you dropped the stuff off."

"Well, you know how it is. There's a couple of girls down there that like me. I kind of, like, lose track of time."

"I ought to dock you a day's pay for that."

"Aw, come on, Chief. You can't do that. I need the money. The women are expensive."

"They can be," Lansing agreed. "Stu, when you cleaned up the crime scene on the other side of the hill, what'd you do with those broken pieces of pottery?"

"What pottery, chief?"

"Remember when we picked up Beau, he had that big, long story about how he and Duke came out here to dig up pottery. I came out the next morning and all I could find was one broken pot."

"Hey, Sheriff," Cortez interrupted. "I got something here."

"Hard or soft."

"It's pretty soft."

"Be careful. That's probably Mr. Longtree."

"Honest, Sheriff," Ortega insisted nervously. "I don't remember any pieces of pots out here."

"Maybe so." Lansing nodded. "Maybe so . . . Be careful with your shovel there. We don't want to damage the corpse. . . ." He paused thoughtfully. "It's strange about that pottery. There was still a piece out here when I came back a couple of days later. I found the rest of the pot on Mack McGaffrey's desk."

"All that old Indian stuff looks the same, Chief." Ortega tried to sound casual. "You know that."

"I suppose." Lansing turned to Carerra. "Margarite, how long did it take you and Elizabeth to drive down to that adobe hut where you found Longtree?"

Carerra shrugged. "Forty, forty-five minutes. Something like that."

"You know, that's amazing, Stu," the sheriff remarked.

"What's that?" The deputy stopped his digging.

"That you managed to drive down to the hut, sift through the rubble to find there was no body, and get back to town in less than an hour."

"I'm sure it took me longer than that!" Ortega protested.

"It didn't . . . because you didn't go. You didn't have to. You already knew what you'd find. That's why you didn't get back to Las Palmas until nine o'clock the day I sent you to Santa Fe. You were up in the hills destroying evidence."

"I told you," Ortega said angrily. "I stopped off and saw some women in town."

"You almost pulled it off, Stu. That was pretty clean, killing Parker in the stables. He was probably the only one left who knew you were involved."

Before Lansing could react, Ortega swung his shovel around, hitting Joe on the side of the head. A second later the deputy had his pistol drawn and pointed at the sheriff.

Lansing tried to shine the light in Ortega's eyes. The deputy simply shot the flashlight out of the sheriff's hand.

"Drop the flashlight, lady!" Ortega yelled. Carerra did as she was told.

Lansing held his hand. It still stung from the gunshot, though he was only grazed.

"I didn't want to kill Parker. I didn't want to kill anyone. But I couldn't let him go and I couldn't bring him in. He had to die."

"What about Longtree? Did you kill him too?"

"Parker did it. I swear it. He cut his throat."

"Why? Why did Longtree have to die?"

"McGaffrey had made him an offer. Help him get control of the strip and Longtree could be a very wealthy man. I guess Longtree told him no."

"So McGaffrey told you to kill him?" Carerra asked.

"No, no. Nobody said anything about killing. Me and Parker followed him and the senator to the strip. When the senator left we went into the hut. Parker asked him one more time if he would take the deal, but Longtree turned him down. Parker told me to hold him. I thought we were going to rough him up. That's when he pulled out the knife."

"So you held him while Parker slit his throat," Lansing said, completing the scene.

"Why did you cut out his heart?" Carerra asked in disgust.

"It was the old Anasazi way, McGaffrey said, before they were driven away. It was the Aztec way. Parker thought the idea of doing it was funny."

"Why'd you try to kill us?" the doctor asked.

"I was scared. I wanted to move the body. Get rid of any evidence I had been there. You were just at the wrong place at the wrong time. It was nothing personal."

"Now what?" Lansing asked.

"I'm sorry, Chief. I didn't want things to turn out this way. If you had just left things alone, everything would have been fine. . . ."

"Drop the gun, Stu. It isn't too late for you."

"Yes, it is. I know what they do to cops in jail and I'm not going."

Cortez looked up at his coworker. "We're your friends. You can't kill us."

"Yes, I can." He pointed the pistol at Cortez's head and pulled the trigger.

At the sound of the gunshot a sudden wind kicked up. Ortega immediately aimed the gun at Lansing. The sand had already started blowing and the deputy had to squint to see. The meager light from the moon was being blocked by flying debris.

"And now, Sheriff, I have to say adios." As he pulled the trigger a handful of sand slammed into his face. Lansing pushed Carerra to the ground and drew his pistol.

Both men shot wildly in the swirling darkness. Lansing emptied his weapon, pointed at the last spot he could remember Ortega standing.

The wind stopped as suddenly as it started, as if a lone dust devil had swept through the ancient ruin and departed. The dim moonlight returned.

Ortega lay still, his body crumpled over the silent form of Joe Cortez.

The sheriff stood, helping Carerra to her feet. They approached Ortega carefully, but they didn't have to worry. The deputy was dead.

They knelt next to the bodies and the doctor checked their pulses. As she did, something caught the corner of Lansing's eye. On the ridge above them, silhouetted against the starry sky, was the frail figure of an old man with long hair.

Lansing looked at the doctor to see if she had seen

him, but when the sheriff turned back the figure had disappeared.

"Did you see him?"

"See who?" Carerra asked, not knowing what he was talking about.

Lansing stared at the vacant ridge, wanting to believe it was more than just his imagination getting the best of him.

"Never mind."

He put his arm around her and led her away from the ruins . . . away from the Anasazi Strip.